**"What is the matter with you?" Raschid rasped, suddenly losing all patience.**

"I thought I told you I didn't want another verbal battle tonight!" Evie snapped right back.

"Then don't turn this into one!" He turned the tables on her as quick as a flash. "You are my life, my heart, my soul, Evie," he added gruffly. "I would do anything for you. I thought you knew that."

"Except marry me," she said.

Harlequin Presents® invites you to see how the other half lives in:

SOCIETY WEDDINGS

*They're gorgeous, they're glamorous... and they're getting married!*

In this sensational five-book miniseries you'll be our VIP guest at some of the most talked-about weddings of the decade— spectacular events where the cream of society gather to celebrate the marriages of dazzling brides and grooms in equally breathtaking international locations.

At each of these lavish ceremonies you'll meet some extra-special men and women—all rich, royal or just renowned!—whose stories are guaranteed to capture your imagination, your heart...and the headlines! For in this sophisticated world of fame and fortune you can be sure of one thing: there'll be no end of scandal, surprises...and passion!

We know you'll enjoy Michelle Reid's **The Mistress Bride.**

Next month, join us in a toast to another happy couple in:
**The Society Groom (#2066)**
by
**Mary Lyons**

# MICHELLE REID

## The Mistress Bride

SOCIETY WEDDINGS

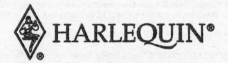

# HARLEQUIN®

TORONTO • NEW YORK • LONDON
AMSTERDAM • PARIS • SYDNEY • HAMBURG
STOCKHOLM • ATHENS • TOKYO • MILAN • MADRID
PRAGUE • WARSAW • BUDAPEST • AUCKLAND

ISBN 0-373-12056-7

THE MISTRESS BRIDE

First North American Publication 1999.

Visit us at www.romance.net

Printed in U.S.A.

# CHAPTER ONE

IT WAS getting late. Almost too late to bother going anywhere now.

Yet Evie stood staring out at London's twinkling night skyline without any outward signs of irritation. After all, there was nothing particularly unusual in her lover keeping her waiting like this; he did it all the time—duty being the altar at which he worshipped, usually at the expense of everything else in his life.

And that included his woman. Beautiful though she might be, special though he might insist she was to him, Evie knew she would always have to take second place to what was really important in his life.

So, like some priceless piece of life-size porcelain draped in sensual blood-red silk, she stood there in front of the drawing-room window in his very luxurious penthouse apartment—and waited. She waited for her man as she had been waiting for the last forty-five minutes now, calmly, patiently.

Or so it might seem, for it wasn't in her nature to show what she was really feeling—a habit drummed into her by a very strict upbringing.

But only fools took that calmness at its serene-faced value.

Sheikh Raschid Al Kadah was nobody's fool, but he wasn't here to note the tell-tale signs to Evie's real mood. And the one person who was attempting to keep her company rarely lifted his eyes high enough to read those signs.

He stood by the white marble fireplace with his hands quietly folded across his robed front and his tongue wisely silent, all attempts at polite conversation abandoned long ago, when apologetically late had become unforgivably late.

He caught her taking a quick glance at her slender gold wristwatch, though. 'I am certain he cannot be many more minutes, Miss Delahaye,' Asim assured her with that quietly soothing diplomatic voice of his. 'Some things are, I am afraid, unavoidable, and a telephone call from his revered father is most definitely one of those things.'

Or a call from New York, Paris or Rome, Evie silently tagged on. The Al Kadah business interests were far-flung and varied. The fact that Raschid, as his father's only son, now shouldered the burden for most of those interests since the old man's minor heart attack last year meant that Evie was seeing less and less of Raschid—her position in the pecking order being as low as it was.

A sigh whispered from her. The kind of sigh she would normally only allow herself when she was sure she was alone. But tonight was different. Tonight she was fretting over a very worrying problem of her own, and she could have done without the added aggravation of a long wait like this when she had, in truth, had to force herself into coming here at all tonight.

Because she knew that Raschid was not going to like what she had to tell him. In fact, she could positively say that he was going to hate it.

Oh, hell, Evie thought heavily, and was just in the process of lifting a decidedly shaky hand to cover the throbbing ache that was taking place behind her eyes when a door at the far end of the room suddenly opened.

The raised hand paused then snapped downwards to form a small fist at her side, her body tensing fractionally as she felt the full stinging impact of Raschid's sharp golden gaze lancing into her slender spine.

A taut silence prevailed as Sheikh Raschid Al Kadah paused in the doorway to his own sumptuous cream and gold living room while sharp shrewd eyes quickly assessed the mood of the room's two occupants. The arrow-straight set of Evie's spine was, to him, eloquent, his servant's clear relief at his arrival profound.

Grimacing slightly in acknowledgement of both, Raschid dismissed the other man with a silent gesture of his head. But the look in Asim's dark eyes spoke volumes as he walked towards him. 'You are in deep trouble, Sheikh,' those wise old eyes told him. 'The lady is not happy.' Asim left them alone with a rather sardonic bow of respect.

Which left only Evie, who was taking her time in turning to face him—a message in itself that he completely misread because he was expecting to see anger, so anger was what he saw in the slow, stiff movement of her body.

Yet, despite her expected irritation and his own weary mood after having just had to endure one of the worst telephone conversations of his entire life with his father, despite the lateness of the hour, and everything else that seemed to be conspiring against him in an effort to turn his complicated life into absolute turmoil—despite all of that, when their eyes actually met down the length of the beautiful white and gold room there was a single sweet moment when everything came to a delicious standstill for both of them. Evie because she was being assailed by that hot, tight burst of sexual awakening that was always her first response to this man. And Raschid because his own response to Evie was no different at all.

The air between them began to pulse, Raschid's eyes darkening with a very possessive sense of pleasure as he stood taking in the shattering impact of Evie's beauty, framed as it was by the darkness outside his apartment window.

So tall, those glittering eyes measured. So incredibly slender yet so beautifully rounded in all the right places. The whole person so inherently sensual to this man who knew every inch of her as intimately as he knew himself.

Skin he knew was as smooth as satin seemed to shine like a pearl against the draping of wine-red silk. Her wonderful hair shone like a coronet of pure gold that had been sleekly contained to frame the most delicately perfect face he had ever seen in his life. Perfect bone structure, perfect nose, perfectly seductive heart-shaped mouth—and those wonderful cold-cut lavender-blue eyes that, even in anger, could not quite disguise what was happening to her as she stood there gazing back at her opposite in every way.

For where her skin was pale his was dark, as dark as lovingly cared for wood that had been honed and planed and carefully polished to create the most exotically beautiful male structure Evie had ever set eyes upon. And if she was tall then he was taller, wider, stronger—tougher. His hair was a smooth, slick, uncompromising black, cut to perfection to make the best of his lethally attractive face—a face with a superbly sculpted long thin nose, acutely defined sensual mouth—and eyes like liquid gold that easily countered cold-cut lavender-blue by seeming to induce her to dive right in.

Opposites—complete and utter opposites. One as English as afternoon tea, the other as Arabian as a Bedouin warrior.

Two years they had been together—two years—and the very air between them could still crackle with that hot, tight sizzle of a fierce sexual awakening that was as strong now as it had been when it began.

But then, it had had to be, or the relationship would not have survived the disapproving rumblings across two very proud cultures.

'My apologies.' Raschid spoke at last and, like the eyes, his voice was so golden it slid over the senses like warm dark honey. 'I have just this moment returned from my embassy.'

Which accounted for his eastern attire, Evie assumed as she ran her cool eyes over the long straight white tunic he was wearing beneath a dark blue, loosely flowing top robe. Though he had delayed long enough to remove his headgear, she noted as she watched a small grimace touch the moulded shape of his mouth at her continuing silence.

'You're angry with me.' Dryly he stated the obvious.

'No,' Evie countered. 'Bored.'

'Ah,' he drawled. 'In one of those moods, are we?' Stepping further into the room, he closed the door. 'What would you like me to do?' he enquired, ever so politely. 'Grovel at your beautiful feet?'

Which was his own unique brand of sarcasm, Evie made rueful note. Quite deliberately she took the words at their face value.

'Right now, I would much rather you feed me,' she replied. 'I haven't eaten since breakfast this morning, and it is now...' she paused to glance at her watch '...almost nine o'clock.'

'So, you do want me to grovel,' he assumed from all of that, not in the least bit fooled by her cold manner.

What he wasn't seeing was the anxiety lurking behind the coldness—thank goodness—because now that she actually had him here in the flesh Evie had cravenly decided she needed time before she said what she had to say to him.

So her barely perceptible shrug sent one of his sleekly defined black silk brows arching, and in two very economical and outwardly innocent gestures war between them was declared. It was not a new aspect of their relationship. In fact the whole foundation of it had been built on a refusal on both parts to pander to the arrogance of the other. Evie refused to pander to his god-like ego and Raschid refused to pander to her ice-princess image.

'I have responsibilities,' he clipped out.

'Really?' Evie drawled.

His eyes began to spark. 'My time is not always my own to do with as I please.'

'So it didn't please you to keep me waiting for almost an hour?' Her turn to use sarcasm, his to respond—or not—depending on his mood.

What he chose to do was to begin walking towards her with the sleek soft tread of a predator ruthlessly stalking its prey. Her nerve-ends began to tighten, sending out electric signals to all parts of her body as she watched him grow in height, in power, in skin-flaying mastery the closer he came to her.

The man was sheer poetry in motion. So lean and lithe and dark and deliciously dangerous that, by the time he came to a stop mere inches away from her, the breath had completely seized in her chest, and tiny tight tingles of a very familiar excitement were beginning to shimmer through her blood.

And this, Evie told herself helplessly, was why she could not bear to consider the prospect of giving up this man.

He touched parts of her no other living being had ever touched.

Liquid gold eyes held iced blue in challenge. A hand with long, lean brown fingers that knew how to be cruel if the moment presented itself came up to take hold of her tilted chin.

'Word of warning,' Raschid murmured softly. 'I am in no mood for temperament tonight. So be wise, my darling, and drop the disgruntled act.'

'But I am disgruntled.' Evie immediately defied the warning. 'You treat me like a lackey and I don't like it.'

'Because I arrive late once in a while?'

'You arrive late more often than you arrive early,' she grimly pointed out.

To her annoyance, his mouth twitched, an unexpected dash of wicked amusement entering the battle. 'And aren't you ecstatic that I am such a latecomer, hmm?' he countered lazily.

It took her a few moments, but when his meaning did manage to sink in Evie sighed, wrenching her chin from his grasp as a wave of pink ran into her cheeks. 'We weren't talking about your sexual prowess!' she admonished.

'Ah,' he sighed. 'That is a great shame.'

'Raschid!' Evie flashed him a look of irritation. 'I'm not—!'

In the mood for this, she had been going to snap at him—but he silenced her with a kiss, his arms snaking around her body and crushing her against him while his arrogant mouth took burning possession of hers.

But the real crime here was that she didn't attempt to make a protest—didn't even pretend to struggle but simply dived right in there with him. She couldn't stop herself. For Raschid tapped a hunger inside her that had not abated in two long years of being fed exclusively by him.

Two years involved in a relationship that had kept their two families pulsing in the background in simmering disapproval, and had kept the world's tabloids waiting with bated breath to see which one of them would eventually end it.

Because it had to end some time, everyone knew that. The heir to a wealthy sheikhdom was expected to marry one of his own one day. While Evie had already blotted her copybook once by turning her back on a marquis to be where she was now. But the pressure was still on for her to do the right thing and marry into her own class— outdated, outmoded and in danger of extinction though that class might be.

But it was the undisputed knowledge that the end was as inevitable as night following day that helped keep their relationship this hot and this fevered.

'So, do we eat or do we continue to fight?' Raschid murmured as his kiss-warmed mouth lifted away from hers.

For 'fight' read 'love', Evie ruefully translated, and knew without a single doubt which one she wanted tonight.

Needed, she thought tragically—oh, how she needed him tonight!

She needed his strength, his dark and driving sensuality. She needed to soak herself in him, drown herself in him— die in him. For this one night she needed to pretend that nothing was different between them. Be the woman he knew and loved so that he could be the man she loved so desperately.

For he was truly all man, this Arabian lover of hers. A man who could make love with just his eyes—as he was doing to her right now. Teasing, knowing, lazily seducing, and so indolently aware of his power over her senses that he didn't need to read the darkened look in her eyes to know how much she wanted him.

'Are you wearing anything at all underneath this?' she asked, playing for time by stroking her palms along the lean, tight contours she could feel beneath the smooth white tunic.

'Why don't you open it and take a look?' he invited, and began nibbling at the corner of her mouth in encouragement while his fingers played tantalisingly with the thin straps that were holding up her dress.

'And have the world and his wife witness your strip show?' she mocked, referring to the fact that they were standing in front of a sheet of well-lit glass through which anyone with reasonable eyesight from Battersea to Westminster would be able to see what they were doing.

His solution to that was to reach over her shoulder. A moment later heavy gold silk brocaded curtains came swishing across the glass, smoothly closing down her options so she had nothing left but a straight choice between demanding he feed her stomach or feed her desire.

Evie would have had to be really stupid not to know what his preference was since it was pushing so prominently against the tingling wall of her stomach, but she also knew he was going to leave the final choice to her. He knew she was angry with him for keeping her waiting. He knew that if he tried to make love to her now without her say-so she was likely to start spitting all kinds of accusations at him about the way he used her.

He also knew that, starving for food or not, in the end she would not be able to resist his seduction. For her own body was also showing the signs of a craving it had never been able to suppress in his vicinity.

'You are so arrogant,' she complained in a last-ditch attempt to hold on to some pride.

He just grinned, all flashing white teeth and pure male confidence. 'Say it,' he prompted, 'or I shall call for Asim to bring the car round.'

On a driven groan of angry frustration, her hands came up between their bodies and took hold of two fistfuls of his blue outer robe. She used it to tug his mouth back to her own. But she punished him by sinking her teeth into his lower lip before she gave him her complete surrender by fusing her hungry body to his.

An hour later Evie came out of a thoroughly satiated daze to find Raschid lying beside her in an indolent sprawl of naked limbs. His eyes were closed, his mouth slightly parted, his breathing a steady rise and fall of a smooth dark gold breastplate liberally smattered with crisp black body hair.

Evie smiled to herself, enjoying the opportunity to lie here like this simply feasting herself on him while he didn't know she was doing it. In fact, looking at a naked and sleepy Raschid had to be one of the best pastimes she had ever experienced. He had a way of lying there that she found unbearably sexy. Arrogant in his nakedness, conceited about his own beauty, so uninhibited in his presentation of his silky dark self that if an army of reporters had suddenly burst into this room he wouldn't have dreamed of covering himself up!

'I need food,' she announced.

'Pick up the phone and call Asim,' he advised, refusing to lift himself out of his satiated stupor.

On a sigh Evie levered herself up on an elbow then stretched across him for the telephone. Her hair, so carefully worked into a sleekly sophisticated pleat not long ago, was now hanging in a curtain of silk that trailed across his cheek as she talked to his personal servant.

'Just a cold sandwich will do,' she was saying when Raschid's hand came up, reaching for the trailing hair to gently comb it behind her ear. 'No. He will eat what I choose to order since he kept me waiting so long,' she said, glancing down to send Raschid a defiant smile. 'And I may just die, Asim, if I have to wait until you cook me something,' she concluded before replacing the phone.

Those liquid eyes were looking at her in a way that had the muscles around her heart tightening like a coiled spring. He was so beautiful, this man, Evie thought helplessly. His soul talked to her soul in a way she knew she could never survive without now.

'Why did you miss out on lunch today?' he asked gravely, his long lean fingers brushing a tender caress across her delicate cheekbone.

'I didn't actually miss out on it,' she confessed. 'I just didn't want to eat what was on offer.'

Raschid frowned. 'Which was—what?'

'Humble pie,' she replied, and rolled away from him, her sigh as she did so the heavy kind that took all the softness he had just spent the last hour loving into existence right away again.

'Explain,' he commanded.

Evie got up, as exquisite to look at naked as she was dressed—and not many women could promise that. Reaching down, she picked up the robe she had recently taken from his body and dragged it over her own. It almost buried her, but she still looked fantastic. With a flick of a hand, she released her hair so it tumbled in a tangle of golden silk down her back—then turned to face him.

'Mother,' she said. That was all. It didn't need an explanation.

And Raschid didn't comment, but his expression became grim, and he sat up to run his fingers through his hair in a gesture of weary frustration while she walked off towards his bathroom, trailing the dark blue robe behind her like a queen with her train.

The bedroom was a masterpiece of interior design, blending two cultures into one with the very modern western use of pale wood floors and furnishings given a touch of the exotic with jewel-coloured silks and priceless Persian carpets.

But the bathroom was sheer Arabian luxury, with bright white and royal blue patterned tile-work covering floors and walls alike. A white enamel sunken tub the size of a plunge pool stood on a dais dead centre of the room. Above it was a dome of mirrored glass that was both wickedly naughty and deliciously decadent. The shower cubical took up enough room for three by normal standards, the gold inlaid double glass doors works of art in themselves.

It was the shower that Evie made for, turning on a tap that sent no less than seven power jets of water sluicing around her at the absolute perfect temperature. She stayed in there for ages, aware of Raschid moving around in the other part of the bathroom.

Aware also that he hadn't come to join her here in the shower because the mood had been ruined. Her mother—his father. It was usually one or the other of them that put this dampener on their pleasure.

But there was worse to come, though Raschid didn't know it yet. Which was why she had walked away just now rather than have it all out with him there and then.

Coward, she accused herself. Then grimaced in acknowledgement of that very obvious fact. But it was not going to be easy to say what she had to say, because the world was about to topple down upon them both, and she didn't know how Raschid was going to react to that.

By the time she left the shower, Raschid had left the bathroom, but a turquoise silk caftan had been draped over a stool and she smiled at his thoughtfulness as she dried herself. She had worn it many times before here. It was one among several Raschid had brought her back from his homeland.

Pulling it on over her naked body, she released her hair from the simple knot she had fastened it in before going into the shower, and the long mass fell in a slightly damp tangle down almost to her waist. Finger-combing it as she moved, she went back into the bedroom to discover that Raschid had gone from there also.

She found him in the living room, standing by the drinks cabinet pouring sparkling water on to freshly squeezed orange juice. Neither of them drank much alcohol, she because she didn't care for it and Raschid because his religion forbade it.

He was dressed, which surprised her. Normally he was hard put to pull on a robe during evenings like this. But that soft checked cotton shirt, buff trousers and casual slip-ons he was wearing on his sockless feet were sending her messages.

Raschid was intending to take her home later rather than keeping her here for the night as he usually would.

Well, maybe that wasn't such a bad idea, Evie told herself heavily when she felt her heart sink in disappointment. For what she had to tell him was going to necessitate some time apart while they both came to terms with what it was going to mean to them.

Hearing her come into the room, he sent her a brief smile over his shoulder. 'Your food has arrived, ma'am,' he drawled. 'Now you may feed that other ravenous appetite of yours.'

It was meant as a joke. But Evie couldn't laugh. Because the moment she glanced across the room to where an elegant soapstone coffee table stood spread out with a cold meal fit for a king her stomach objected.

Having gone from clutching at her with a demand to be fed, it was now clutching with sickening dread because she knew she couldn't put it off any longer.

'Raschid,' she said huskily. 'I need to talk to you.'

Glass in hand, he turned, something in her tone perhaps alerting him to trouble, because his eyes had already sharpened. 'What?' he demanded.

Her throat dried up, her eyes shifting away from him because she knew she couldn't look at him and say what she had to say. So instead she walked over to the window where she reached out to send the curtain swishing open so she could fix her gaze on something outside while she decided how to begin.

A tense silence followed. One where Evie could feel Raschid's quick mind grinding into action, picking up on the vibrations she was giving off, sorting through them and—belatedly perhaps—realising that all was not well with his lover.

After a minute, he put down his glass and walked slowly towards her. He didn't attempt to touch her—those shrewd instincts of his warning him that she needed her own space.

'What's wrong, Evie?' he prompted soberly.

Tears washed across her eyes and stayed there. 'We have a problem,' she began huskily—only to go silent again when she found she couldn't continue.

Raschid said nothing, waiting patiently for her to go on. Evie could see his face reflected in the darkened window. He looked grave, the smoothly handsome lines of his features so very still that she knew he had already prepared himself for something dire to come.

And, to her wretched despair, she found she couldn't do it. He was too important to her. She loved him so deeply that she discovered she couldn't risk the chance of losing him.

Not yet, she thought achingly. Please, not yet.

'My mother wants you to find an excuse not to attend my brother's wedding,' she said, dragging the half-truth out from the depths of a real desperation.

Another silence. Evie watched that face via its darkened reflection and saw a frown mar its smooth lines. Her heart began to beat with a sickly pump. He wasn't a fool, this man of hers. His highly tuned instincts where she was concerned had been warning him of something far more disastrous than a silly problem with her mother.

Oh, there was truth in the lie, she grimly acknowledged as she stood there waiting for his response. Her mother had spent the whole of their lunch together today telling Evie in no uncertain terms how much she would prefer it if Sheikh Raschid stayed away from Julian's high-profile wedding in two weeks' time.

'The notoriety that the two of you generate is bound to shift emphasis away from the bride and groom and on to yourselves,' Lucinda Delahaye had predicted. 'If he had the smallest amount of sensitivity he would have realised that himself and graciously declined the invitation. But since he has no sensitivity I feel it is your place to tell him.'

But, as both Raschid and her mother knew, Evie was not open to that kind of petty manipulation. Under normal circumstances she wouldn't have even bothered mentioning such a conversation to Raschid.

So, what had been normal about today? she asked herself starkly as she watched that reflected face shift from puzzlement into annoyance. Within minutes of her getting up this morning the whole day had gone rocketing out of control. Since then she'd felt as if she'd been in a car accident, so shocked and dazed that she'd been barely able to function on a normal level.

In fact, the whole day had gone by in a fog. Until Raschid had taken her to bed of course, she mused ruefully. There the fog had cleared up remarkably—only to be replaced with a different kind of fog.

The glorious fog of loving.

Now even that fog had cleared, she noted heavily, and Raschid was standing behind her looking as if she had really let him down after such a tense build-up.

Which was, in effect, what she had just done.

'Is that it?' he said eventually.

'Yes,' she confirmed, pitifully aware of the depth of her own wretched cowardice.

'Then go to hell,' he murmured succinctly, refusing the request without any compunction. And turned his back on her to walk away.

Her heart took a lurching leap to her throat. The way he had said that told her he knew she had just chickened out over something. She turned too, staring anxiously after him as he crossed the room with that long, lithe, graceful stride of his that always set her pulses racing no matter what the mood was like between them.

'Raschid, you—'

'I refuse to discuss it,' he cut in, sounding annoyed, offended and just downright disgusted, which made Evie wonder how he would have reacted to what she had cravenly backed out from saying. 'Your mother is not your keeper and she certainly isn't mine!'

'It's a fair request,' she said, surprising herself by jumping to the defence of her mother. It seemed that anything was better than confessing the truth, she ruefully acknowledged. 'You know as well as I do the kind of interest we generate when we go anywhere together. In this case, it has to be Julian and Christina my mother must consider, not your feelings or mine.'

'And my father is a very close friend of Christina's father,' Raschid coldly countered. 'In fact, Lord Beverley is almost solely responsible for helping my father overcome some very awkward political and diplomatic obstacles in his quest to reform and modernise my country. I will not offend Christina's father simply because your mother wants me to.'

The chin was up, Evie noted. The passionate lover was now in full Noble Prince mode.

'In the face of my father's failing health,' Prince Raschid concluded, 'it is my duty to be there as my father's representative.'

Duty. Evie knew all about Raschid's dedication to duty! It was a shame that sense of duty did not extend to encompass the woman who was his lover.

'So be it,' she said, suddenly sounding as cold as ever she could sound when she felt like it. 'But don't be surprised if I put into place some contingency plans of my own to keep the gossip to its minimum.'

His eyes narrowed on her. 'What's that supposed to mean?'

Evie shrugged. 'Duty,' she quoted right back at him. 'I have a duty to ensure that my brother and his bride maintain centre stage on the day of their wedding.'

'And how do you intend to do that?' he mocked her. 'By pretending I don't exist?'

'Would you notice if I did?' Evie threw back cynically.

She could have bitten off her tongue when his sharp eyes narrowed. 'Was that it?' he demanded. 'Was that remark a big hint to what is actually eating at you tonight, Evie?' He clarified the question. 'That I don't give you enough of my attention?'

So he had guessed that she'd just dissembled. Evie smiled to herself and wondered how he would react if she told him he couldn't be any further from the truth.

'Would you care that much if it was?' she countered, throwing him yet another red herring.

He didn't answer—which was, she supposed bleakly, an answer in itself.

'I'm tired,' she said wearily. 'I think I'll go home...'

Which was just another provoking remark he let float pointedly by him. 'I have to go away tomorrow,' he informed her instead. 'I will be gone for about a week. When I get back I think we need to talk.'

Evie shivered, feeling the icy fingers of a terrible foreboding go trailing down her spine. 'Fine,' she said, moving towards the door.

He said not a word, but his eyes did as they followed her passage across the room. He was sharp, he was shrewd, he had a mind like a multi-million-dollar computer that was programmed to make very accurate assessments at lightning speed.

He knew as well as she knew that there was something going on here that she wasn't telling him.

'Evie...'

He was a master of timing, too, Evie tagged on to her list of attributes as she paused in the doorway. She didn't turn, and the silence between them lengthened like a wire being stretched to its absolute limit. Unspoken emotions beating out a throbbing tattoo that made her want to just break down, right here and now, and sob her wretched heart out.

'I would care,' he murmured gruffly.

It was too much. On a whisper of silk, Evie turned and ran to him.

I love you so very much, she wanted to cry out, but didn't dare in case the evocative words started the avalanche she knew would bury that love without a single trace.

So instead she wrapped her arms around him and buried her misery in the warmth of his solid presence.

I'll tell him after Julian's wedding, she promised herself weakly. It can easily wait until then...

# CHAPTER TWO

IT HAD been billed as the wedding of the year, and anyone who was anyone was expected to be there to watch Sir Julian Delahaye and Lady Christina Beverley tie the sacred knot: the rich, the famous, titled nobility, not to mention a heavy presence of foreign dignitaries who had flown in from all over the world to be here—out of respect for Christina's father, whose diplomatic skills had earned him lifelong friends in far-flung places.

The weather was glorious, the location a picture-perfect English castle complete with ramparts and moat set in its very own ten-thousand-acre estate right in the heart of Royal Berkshire.

You really couldn't get any more romantic than that. It was no wonder some people were willing to sell their souls to acquire an invitation.

Which made Evie very much the odd one out here today, because she would have sold her soul to be anywhere but here.

She should, in fact, have been heading up an entourage of six lovely bridesmaids. You could even say that it had been expected of her. But she'd turned the invitation down, upsetting several and annoying many, but...

A sigh broke from her—the pair of lavender-blue eyes staring back at her via the dressing-table mirror she was sitting in front of mocking to say the least.

She just couldn't have done it to the happy couple. After all, how much bad luck did you invite on yourself by having the family black sheep play a major role at your marriage? It just wouldn't do and they all knew it wouldn't do—which was why Christina's mother had found it

23

difficult to hide her relief when Evie had turned the request down.

But neither did it mean she could escape her duty altogether. As sister to the groom she had an obligation to be here—if only for Julian's sake. And, black sheep of the family or not, she was not about to disappoint her brother. She loved and respected him too much.

So here she was, quietly preparing herself for the event ahead, in the room allotted to her by the Beverley family in the east wing of their beautiful home—very much aware that her mother was doing the same in another room not that far away, because she could feel the waves of resentment reaching out to her through several layers of solid stone.

And why was her mother so resentful? Evie asked that pair of eyes in the mirror. Because Lady Lucinda Delahaye had once been thwarted of the chance to put on a day like this for her own daughter when Evie had turned her back on the chance to marry a marquis so she could be with her lover.

'He won't marry you!' her mother had angrily predicted two years ago. 'He's an Arab prince for goodness' sake! And unlike you he will know his duty! When the time comes he will turn his back on you and marry one of his own. You mark my words, Evie. You mark my words.'

Well, she'd marked them all right—and to this very day she was still marking them. Though the moment of their parting now loomed so very large on the horizon that it actually blocked out her view of anything else.

Two weeks you've had—two long wretched weeks to find enough courage to tell Raschid what he needs to be told, she castigated those mocking eyes in the mirror. And what do you do? You avoid him. You let him fly home to Behran for a week without saying a single thing, then spend the next week not even daring to let yourself see him.

Excuses—excuses. Her life recently had become one long round of lying excuses.

Another sigh whispered from her, one of those heavy sighs she had caught herself releasing a lot recently. She looked bruised around the eyes, she noticed, even with the very professional job she had done on her make-up. But then, a worry and lack of sleep had a habit of doing that.

Coward, she derided those eyes in the mirror.

A knock sounding at the door to her room forced her to put her thoughts aside as she turned on her dressing stool to invite whoever was there to come in. The heavy oak door swung smoothly inwards on well-oiled hinges, and her brother Julian stepped into the room.

He looked gorgeous, already dressed in his formal grey morning suit with its dashing silver silk waistcoat and cravat.

'Hi,' he greeted. 'How are you feeling?'

'It should be me asking you that question,' Evie smiled.

His answering shrug showed that Julian was not in the least bit nervous about what was to come. He loved Christina to distraction and Christina openly adored him. This was no carefully arranged union between two noble dynasties.

'Mother's having a panic attack over the state of her hat or some such thing,' he drawled. 'So I thought I would come and hide in here.'

'You're welcome,' Evie murmured, following him with wryly understanding eyes as he went to stand by her window.

Their mother could be an absolute tyrant when she was stressed out or angry. Today she would be feeling stressed out, worrying that she didn't let the family down, that her choice of outfit was absolutely perfect, that she looked exactly what she was—the upper-class super-elegant mother of the handsome baronet groom.

'I can't believe they've stuck you right out here on the

edge of the world,' Julian complained, checking out the view she had of the stable block that had been temporarily turned into a car park.

The vast fifty-bedroom castle had been split into two pieces for the wedding, the east wing housing guests of the groom while the guests of the bride occupied the west wing. The further east you went, the smaller the rooms became until—this one, where the old tester bed almost filled it and the plumbing was antiquated—a message in itself to the dreaded black sheep.

Smiling to herself, Evie turned back to the mirror. 'I have been put here because this is so obviously a single room,' she explained, using the exact same words Christina's stiffly smiling mother had used when she'd shown her in here earlier that morning. 'And I am so obviously a single woman,' she tagged on in mockery of herself.

'They're all such damned hypocrites,' Julian grunted in disgust. 'They might disapprove of you and what you do in your private life, but they don't have to be so obvious about it. I wouldn't mind,' he added, 'but they had the damned barefaced cheek to invite him!'

'Not for my benefit.'

'No,' her brother acknowledged grimly. 'They invited him because they can't afford to offend him—despite what he is to you.'

'And he had the damned bad taste to accept,' Evie said.

'Your doing?' Julian asked.

'No,' she denied, her voice cooling considerably because she'd wondered if Julian had been suspecting her of trying to manipulate the situation. 'Actually, I asked him not to come.'

And he told me to go to hell, she recalled with a weary grimace. Not that she had expected anything less from him. Raschid was arrogant by birth. It was built into his genes to ignore what it did not suit him to see.

And refusing to see his presence here today as an embarrassment to her stupid mother was, perhaps, one of his more understandable bouts of blindness. After all who, in this day and age, condemned a man and woman for wanting to be together so long as they were both free and single?

Free and single, she repeated wryly to herself. What a worn-out cliché. For there was nothing free in the way she and Raschid conducted their relationship. It had cost them both dearly in family respect and personal privacy. And she hadn't felt single since the day she met him, which explained why she had put off telling him what she knew she had to tell him one day.

But not today, she told herself as she glanced around at her brother. For today belonged to Christina and this precious brother of hers—who was standing there with his back to her, his hands thrust into his trouser pockets in what she considered his disgruntled pose.

Which meant he was cross, and she didn't want him looking cross. She didn't want him looking anything but happy today—for they would only blame her if he did.

'Hey,' she said, getting up to go and link her arm through one of his. 'Stop grouching,' she scolded. 'It spoils your handsome features.'

He turned a rakish grin on her. Her heart swelled to bursting because she so loved this big brother of hers who she knew loved her unreservedly in return.

'You look stunning,' Julian murmured softly. 'I love the dress.'

'Thank you,' she smiled. 'I bought it specially for the occasion.'

And to make a statement—a rather obvious statement that announced to everyone that, although she was not playing a major role at this wedding, neither was she about to fade into the background as she was sure most of them would prefer her to do.

The dress was short and it was clingy, made of a fine silk jersey material that moulded every slender line of her body from shoulder to well above the knee and so left more than enough of her wonderful legs on show. It was also red. A dramatically unapologetic letterbox-red, with a scooped neck, and a thin gold belt that hugged her narrow waistline. On her feet she was wearing very high-heeled strappy gold sandals, and waiting for her on the bed was a tiny bolero jacket in the same red as the dress.

Plus her hat—a wide and floppy-brimmed gold gauzy affair, bought to use as a prop to hide her thoughts and feelings beneath while she got herself through what promised to be one hell of an ordeal of a day.

'They certainly won't miss the fact that you're here,' Julian observed. Her brother was no fool; he knew what she was trying to do here.

'The wicked lady in red,' she grinned. 'I can't fight them so I have no choice but to join them in condemning myself.'

'Will he mind you taking them on in public like this?' he asked curiously.

Evie's slender shoulders lifted and fell in a gesture of indifference. 'He may be my lover but he is not my keeper.'

'Ah. I scent trouble in the air,' Julian sighed. 'Is this his punishment for refusing to stay away?'

She didn't answer, her hand sliding away from his arm so she could go back to the dressing table and finish getting ready. There was a moment's silence, the kind taut with words she didn't want him to utter.

'Evie—'

'No,' she cut in. 'Don't start, Julian. Not today of all days; I'm just not up to it.'

'But—'

'But nothing,' she inserted firmly. 'What goes on between Raschid and myself is our business. Keep out of it.'

'Well, that's telling me,' he drawled after a moment. 'Makes me wonder what you told our dear mother...'

'Is that why you're here, Julian?' she sighed. 'To find out if it was me who put her in a temper?'

'Was it?' he asked.

'I haven't even seen her since she drove me down here this morning.'

'And she didn't have a go at you then?'

'We had guests with us,' Evie explained.

'That's it, then.' Julian nodded sagely. 'Poor old thing is feeling frustrated because she's not had a chance to deliver the big lecture.'

'You mean the one about nicely brought up young ladies not sleeping with wicked Arabs?' Evie enquired innocently while applying a touch of mascara to her lashes.

'She's such a social snob,' Julian sighed.

'Not a social snob, Julian. A cultural snob,' Evie amended. 'If she were just a social snob she would be pulling out all the stops possible to get the dreadful Arab to marry me—a genuine prince with more money than sense being better than an impoverished marquis—socially speaking.'

'Actually—' Julian grimaced '—I wasn't referring to that lecture. I was referring to the one about the two of you not showing the family up by openly fawning all over each other today.'

Surprisingly Evie let out a laugh, her eyes suddenly alight with sardonic merriment as she looked at her brother via the mirror. 'The day hasn't arrived when you'll see Raschid fawning over anyone—in public or out of it!' she said. 'He's too damned arrogant. Too aware of his own worth to stoop that low. Odd really,' she added thoughtfully, 'that Mother can't stand the sight of him, because they're two of a kind in that respect.'

'You make it sound as if you dislike the man,' Julian murmured dryly.

Dislike him? She adored him, Evie admitted silently. It was herself she didn't like very much. 'He's great in bed,' she offered as a light diversion from where this conversation was threatening to lead her.

Another knock sounded on her bedroom door then, and both brother and sister turned to watch the door swing open—and their mother step gracefully inside.

Tall like themselves, slender and fair like themselves, she looked the most stylish mother-of-the-groom that had ever been presented, in a pale blue and cream suit that shrieked classical Chanel.

'I thought I would find you here, Julian,' she said. 'Your guests are beginning to arrive. And it's time for you to be taking your place.'

In other words, she wanted to be alone with Evie so she could deliver the expected lecture. Julian opened his mouth to warn her off the idea, felt Evie's hand give his arm a warning pinch—and reluctantly smothered the urge.

He knew as well as Evie did that to upset their mother today of all days was just asking for trouble.

So with a shrug and a kiss dropped fondly on Evie's cheek he took his leave, though he was unable to do it without issuing a warning of his own as he passed by his mother. Not with words, but the cool look in his eyes had his mother's lashes fluttering downwards and her mouth staying shut as he left, closing the door behind him.

The air in the room suddenly felt very frosty. 'Is that what you're wearing?' Lucinda Delahaye enquired.

Evie sucked in a deep breath of air then let it out again carefully before replying. 'Yes.'

Disapproval was rife in the kind of expression her mother had perfected beautifully. 'It isn't quite what I would call appropriate, Evie. Couldn't you have come up with something less—eye catching?'

'I promise not to outshine Christina,' Evie vowed with a smile that didn't reach her eyes. 'But you look wonderful, Mother,' she added. 'The epitome of grace and style in fact.'

'Yes…' Lucinda Delahaye drawled and walked over to her daughter's wardrobe, leaving that single word to hang in the air between them as a cutting reference to her daughter's lack of both.

Evie looked on mutely as her mother opened the wardrobe door then stood eyeing its few contents in silent disfavour. Evie knew what she was doing, of course; she was searching for an alternative to the red dress—which was why Evie had made sure she had nothing else with her she could wear to her brother's wedding.

She had been through scenes similar to this before, after all.

'There is nothing here for the grand ball tonight,' her mother remarked finally.

Evie stared across the room at this woman who was her mother—and sadly wondered if she would ever learn to forgive her daughter for falling in love with the wrong man. She supposed not, she conceded bleakly. Especially not while her mother could blind her eyes to the exquisite length of spun gold silk hanging in the wardrobe that had Raschid and the East written all over it.

He had brought it back with him from a visit home a couple of months ago. 'I saw this when I took Ranya shopping, and immediately thought of you,' he'd explained.

Ranya was Raschid's sister with whom Evie felt very intimate—though she had never so much as clapped eyes on her. But she was the same age as Evie and maybe because of that Raschid talked about her a lot. He admired Ranya's unquestioning sense of duty—but whether Raschid also admired the way Ranya's husband kept a mistress tucked away here in London Evie wasn't sure. He tended to go all stiff and eastern on her when she brought up the subject—usually in the middle of a row—and their rows tended to be about their respective families' disapproval of their relationship.

But the dress really was a sensational creation, made of gossamer-fine pure silk chiffon that seemed to drip to the floor like gold-spangled toffee. Long-sleeved, low-necked and gathered at the waist, it had a way of moving in opposition to her body that was intensely alluring.

'Don't be a bore, Mother,' Evie said wearily, sighing. 'Skirting around the subject of Raschid is not going to make him go away, you know.'

'Then what will?'

Startled because there had been a definite note of wry sardonicism in her mother's tone then, Evie glanced warily at her—saw the wryness was showing in her eyes as well—and matched it with a similar look of her own.

'Nothing while I can hardly bear to be apart from him,' she answered fatalistically.

Which made it her mother's turn to sigh and she walked over to the window to stand, staring bleakly out at the unremarkable view much as Julian had done a few minutes before her.

And on a stab of remorse because—again like Julian—Evie did not want to see her mother looking anything but radiant today she went to brush a gentle kiss across her delicately perfumed cheek.

'I love you, darling,' she murmured softly.

'But you love him more.' Her mother grimaced.

There really was no answer to that except the truth and Evie wisely decided to keep that to herself. 'I promise faithfully,' she said instead, 'that I will do nothing today that could embarrass you.'

Her mother nodded, for once taking Evie at her word, and as a gesture of gratitude for that Evie dropped another kiss on her mother's cheek before she moved over to the bed to collect her bolero.

'Harry's here.'

Evie's fingers stilled on the tiny red jacket. 'Yes,' she answered quietly. 'I know.'

'He never did get over you.'

'He will,' she assured her. 'Given time and the right woman.'

'*You* were the right woman,' Lucinda turned to flash at her. 'Have you spoken to him since you jilted him?' she then asked curiously.

'I didn't jilt him!' Evie denied. 'He asked me to marry him. I turned him down,' she snapped, her patience beginning to wear thin. 'Harry graciously accepted that refusal two years ago—why can't you do the same thing, Mother?'

'Because I still have this picture of the two of you happy together until Sheikh Raschid came along and ruined it!'

'He may have ruined your plans,' Evie said impatiently, 'but he certainly didn't ruin mine! I love Raschid!' She declared her feelings outright. 'I adore him! I bless each new day that I am allowed to spend in his life! Does that say it clearly enough for you?'

'And when the day comes that he no longer wants you in his life?' her mother challenged, undeterred. 'What will you have left, Evie, tell me that?'

More than you can envisage right now, Evie thought tragically. 'Why can't you just be happy that I am happy?' she cried.

'Because you aren't happy,' her mother countered. 'In fact, Evie,' she added, 'I would say that recently you have looked anything but happy! Would you like to tell me why that is, considering this wonderful love affair you're so blissfully involved in?'

It showed? 'I don't know what you're talking about,' she said, turning away before her mother could read her shock for exactly what it was.

'No?' her mother quizzed. 'Well...' she began walking back to the door '...I suppose we will soon know the truth in that. Just make sure you don't make too much of your affair with him in front of everyone today,' she added curtly—which was what she'd really come in here to say in the first place. 'There will be representatives from all the Arab states present. I don't want my daughter's name being bandied around the Middle East as some notoriously loose woman.'

Loose woman? Oh, good grief! Evie watched the door close behind her mother's retreating back and wanted to throw something after her!

But instead she sank down on to the end of the bed and wilted like a weary flower.

This, she predicted, was going to be one hell of a day to get through!

And not only because of her mother's stuffy attitude, but because she knew she was going to have to run the gauntlet of all those other disapproving faces that were waiting for her out there today—and that went for Arab and English alike!

Damn you, Raschid, she thought. For being who you are and what you are. And damn herself for being who and what she was, she then added heavily. For if only one of them had been a simple nobody, their relationship wouldn't cause a single bat of a single eyelid!

But he had to be the wonderful heir to one of the noblest families in Arabia and she had to be the daughter of one of England's oldest names. And even those two points together were not worrying enough to excite all the trouble their relationship incited. No, it was the very disturbing fact that the relationship had been standing firm for so long that caused rumblings of discontent on all sides.

Rumblings that were in real danger of becoming major eruptions in the near future, Evie mused bleakly.

'Damn,' she breathed. 'Damn, damn, damn.' And got to her feet so she could finish getting herself ready to face the day.

# CHAPTER THREE

OUTSIDE the magnificent sandstone castle, the sleek lawns running down from the moat to a beautiful natural lake had been taken over by caterers. A giant marquee now obliterated the view of the lake from the castle itself, while inside the grand ballroom had been transformed into a flower-strewn love-bower—just in case the weather decided to turn inclement.

But Mother Nature was being very obliging today. The sun was shining, and the soft summer air was heavy with the scent of roses and resonant with the sound of a military brass band playing catchy medleys of popular classics from its allocated corner of the lawn.

Roll upon roll of protective green carpet had been laid out across the grass to form walkways from the house to the marquee and marquee to the separate canopy where the marriage itself was to take place in what had to be an inspired piece of forward planning.

For, because there were far too many guests to make the use of the Beverleys' private chapel a viable proposition today, a huge white canvas canopy had been erected and extended right over the top of the old stone archway that formed the entrance to the chapel grounds. Just inside the arch a stone altar had been erected. Beyond that the brightly coloured stained-glass window of the chapel itself formed the perfect backdrop for the couple when they exchanged their vows on what would be in effect consecrated ground.

Everyone was very impressed.

Even Evie, who had deliberately left it as late as she could before coming outside, though she was not so late that everyone had taken their seats ready for the bride and her entourage to make their entrance.

People were still standing around in the sunshine talking, smiling, laughing, joking. Famous people. Important people. People from all over the world, mingling to form a myriad of colour in the bright sunlight. People who, for once, didn't mind posing for the half dozen official photographers circulating in their midst, even though some of those photographers belonged to the press—allowed in by special invitation and warned to be unobtrusive—or else.

The atmosphere had a warm, festive quality to it that brought a smile to Evie's lips as she made her way along the green carpet pathway towards the open canopy. People glanced up, smiled, said hello, brushed their lips against her cheek if they knew her well enough, shook her hand if they didn't. Or some simply gazed upon her in curious speculation because, despite what she had promised her mother about not outshining the bride today, Evangeline Delahaye could not help but stand out as someone very special.

She was tall, she was slender, she was stunningly lovely. And she was the famous lover of an Arab prince—a man with more wealth and power at his fingertips than most people here could even imagine. He was also gorgeous—which added even more spice to the affair because it made the whole thing so deliciously romantic.

It was the love affair of the decade. The press adored it; their respective families hated it. And everyone else liked to speculate on what the future held for them. While the couple themselves ignored all and everything that was said about them—whether that be by the enthusiastic press or their disapproving families.

Which in turn placed them in the dubious position of being the curiosities at functions like this. Especially when it was so absolutely obvious that they were both here today but not as a couple.

He was here in his official capacity as representative of Behran, she in her role as sister to the groom.

'May I take your photograph, Miss Delahaye?'

Glancing around, Evie saw the eager face of a young man who was a photographer for a well-known broadsheet. He was smiling expectantly, camera at the ready and relaxed because everyone here today had been so accommodating.

But: 'Thank you—no.' Evie refused politely. And kept on walking until she stepped beneath the wedding canopy.

Some people were already in their places. Her brother for instance, still looking impressively at ease as he stood talking to his best man and oldest friend, Sir Robert Malvern, while her mother sat in the row of chairs behind him, listening intently to whatever Great-Aunt Celia was saying to her.

Lecturing her on how to deal with me, most probably, going by the fierce expression on the old lady's face, Evie assumed. And moved her bland blue gaze onwards—until she reached the other side of the aisle—and inevitably, maybe, found Raschid.

Her heart stopped beating momentarily, the studied blandness softening out of her eyes as they soaked in this man who gave her life meaning.

He was standing within a group of his own people, all Arab dignitaries from different Arab states wearing traditional Arab attire. But to her there was only one man standing there. In height, in looks, in sheer masculine charisma he reigned supreme over everyone. He was wearing white, the formal white silk *dishdasha* of his royal office, with its gold sash wrapped around his whipcord-lean waist, and triple gold bands around the plain white *gutra* that covered his head.

And he seemed to sense the precise moment that her eyes came to rest on him because—despite the fact that he seemed engrossed in whatever the man beside him was saying to him—his head lifted and he looked directly at her. Their eyes clashed and for those few brief moments out of time neither moved a single muscle as their usual reaction to each other held them transfixed in a private world of their own.

They did not openly acknowledge each other, though, neither by word nor by gesture. But it was clear that there had to be some way they were communicating, because the vibrations suddenly assailing the humid air beneath the canopy had everyone else going utterly silent.

Heads swivelled, eyes growing curious as they flicked from her face to his face then back again. Julian noticed the thickening silence, glanced up, saw and grimaced ruefully. But his mother's cheeks went pink with anger. She abruptly turned her back on what she saw as her daughter making a spectacle of them—while the Arab standing next to Raschid touched his arm and murmured something to regain his attention.

It broke the spell. Raschid lowered his eyes to listen to what his companion was saying to him and Evie slid her cool blue gaze back to where her great-aunt was now glowering at her in pursed-lipped disapproval.

After that Evie and Raschid completely ignored one another. Evie went to have a quiet word with her brother before taking her place next to her mother, while behind them the makeshift church slowly filled up as the rest of the guests began to filter in from outside.

By the time a rather flustered and watery-eyed Lady Beverley was escorted to her place by one of the ushers, the congregation had fallen into a tense, waiting silence.

Then suddenly, piped out to them from the depths of the small chapel, an organ began to play. The sound of a wedding march filled the canopy at the same time as several gasps from the back rows heralded the arrival of the bride.

And Evie couldn't resist turning in her seat to see a

vision in white come gliding slowly down the aisle on her proud father's arm.

Christina looked utterly enchanting in a flowing off-the-shoulder gown made of the most exquisite Chantilly lace that was such a perfect foil for her dark-haired beauty. In her hair she wore a band of pale pink roses—the same pink roses that made up her bouquet and were an exact match in colour to the pretty organza dresses worn by her five bridesmaids who followed behind.

And she was smiling. Christina was so sure of her love for Julian and his love for her that there wasn't a single sign of wedding nerves in her.

It was that which brought a lump to Evie's throat as she turned to look at her brother to see the exact same expression of pleasure and pride written on his face as he stood there watching his bride come towards him.

I wish…she found herself thinking wistfully, and was glad that Raschid was sitting several rows back from her so he couldn't see her expression.

Would he sense it, though? she wondered. Was he sitting there witnessing this very English marriage and comparing what Christina and Julian were doing here with what could never be for them?

They loved each other; Evie didn't for one moment doubt that love. And in a way she and Raschid had made louder statements about that love by upholding it in the face of so much dissension.

But loving boldly and pledging oneself to that love before God held no comparison. For one was a solemn vow of commitment as legal and spiritually binding as life itself—whereas the other would always be a tenuous thing without that legal commitment, without the blessing, no matter what the God.

'We are gathered here today to witness the joining of this man and this woman in holy matrimony…'

Beside her, she felt her mother stir as she lifted a lace-

edged handkerchief to dab a tear from her eye. Guilt struck
a sudden blow directly at Evie's heart. The guilt of a child
who was starkly aware of what a disappointment she was
to her parent because Lucinda would never feel the pride
and satisfaction that Christina's mother must be feeling
right now, as she watched her daughter marry well and
proudly.

Oh, damn, Evie thought, feeling utterly depressed suddenly. And on an act of impulse she reached out to grasp
her mother's hand. Lifting it to her lips, she kissed it
gently—she didn't know why—unless it was in mute apology.

Whatever, her mother rejected the gesture by firmly re-
moving her hand.

Which hurt—hurt so badly that Evie was barely aware
of what went on for the rest of the ceremony as she became
lost in a bleak little world of her own faults and failures.

Her failure as a daughter being only one of them. For
she had failed someone else here today—though he didn't
know that.

Yet.

Prayers, blessings, hymns, vows—Evie responded
where expected of her without really knowing she was
doing it. In a kind of self-defence she had blanked herself
off from everything, walled herself behind a bland smile
and glassy blue eyes that only a few people here today
would be able to tell were hiding a worryingly unhappy
woman.

Sheikh Raschid Al Kadah was one of those people. He
sat several rows back and to one side of her with his head
lowered for most of the service—whilst his senses were
picking up the kind of vibrations that made his blood run
cold.

She appeared tranquil, he observed, taking a brief glance
at her under cover of coming to his feet for the singing of
a hymn. Her exquisite profile looked as composed as it

always was when in public. Her fingers were relaxed, her
body revealing no jerky movements that could hint towards tension.

Yet every single highly tuned instinct he possessed
where Evie was concerned was telling him a completely
different story.

It had to be this damned wedding, he blamed. For what
woman didn't dream of joining herself in marriage to the
man she loved as Christina Beverley was doing today?

What man would turn down the opportunity to legally
bind himself to a woman like Evie if he had the chance to
do it?

He shifted restlessly, feeling a wave of angry discontent
sweep through him at his own inability to make her feel
more secure in his life.

He was heartily glad when the service was over and
everyone relaxed a little as the couple went off with their
entourage towards the chapel itself where the register was
apparently signed. It wasn't often he found himself yearn-
ing for alcohol but this moment was surely one of them.

'On the face of it,' his companion observed beside him,
'if you remove the religious inferences, a Christian marriage is not so very different from our own.'

You wouldn't be saying that if it was me marrying Evie,
Raschid thought caustically through the fixed smile he offered in wordless acknowledgement.

The band suddenly struck up again, followed by the dul-
cet tones of a solo tenor, saving him the need to offer a
polite reply.

Instead, he flicked a hooded glance back to Evie again.
She was sitting straight-backed now, most definitely tense,
listening to whatever the old lady in the lilac dress was
saying so severely. Her mother had gone, joining the rest
of the bridal party to watch the signing ceremony—from
which, it seemed, Evie had been excluded.

By her own choice, he knew that, but it didn't make

him feel any better for hearing her voice in his head saying, 'Imagine the headline beneath the wedding photograph, Raschid, if I took a major role in this wedding: "Evangeline Delahaye plays chief bridesmaid at her brother's wedding while her Arab prince lover looks on!"' she'd quoted caustically. 'Not "Lady Christina Beverley marries Sir Julian Delahaye at her beautiful Berkshire home"!' she'd concluded. 'I refuse to steal their thunder, and that's the end of it.'

Which was also why she had asked him not to attend today and—arrogant as always—he had treated the request with the contempt he believed it had deserved.

But now, as he sat here witnessing the way Evie had been isolated from something she should have been allowed to share, he began to realise just how selfish he had been.

The old lady in the lilac dress was scowling, he noticed. Her wizened mouth spitting words at Evie who was sitting there with her lovely head lowered as she listened. Then the head lifted suddenly and turned. She had time only to speak one single word, but whatever that word was the old lady launched herself to her feet, sent Evie one last hostile volley then she stalked angrily away to go and sit herself down several rows back. Leaving Evie entirely alone.

The desire to get up and go over there, sit with her—declare his support for this woman whose only sin was in loving the wrong man—almost overwhelmed him. Except he knew she wouldn't want that, for it would only cause the one thing she was trying so hard to avoid here.

Talk, gossip, speculation—shifting the centre of attention away from the bride and groom and on to themselves.

But, damn it, she looked so wretchedly deserted sitting there on her own like that! And something very close to a desire to commit bloody murder exploded in his chest—aimed directly at himself for his own lousy inadequacies as the lover of such a beautiful and special woman.

Evie could feel the sting of curious eyes on her as her great-aunt stalked away. It took everything she had in her to maintain an outwardly calm composure while inside she felt as if she was being eaten up by a million ravenous worms.

'And there he sits, surrounded by his own kind,' her great-aunt had hissed at her. 'Pretending to be civilised when really he is nothing better than a womanising barbarian!'

Evie would have found the words funny if she'd dared. But Great-Aunt Celia hadn't finished with her at that point, and the next volley that left the old lady's lips had not been funny at all. 'While you, you brazen little hussy, insult the Delahaye name the way you carry on with him! Do you have no shame?' she'd demanded.

'No,' Evie had quite coolly replied.

And that was the point where the old lady had stormed off, leaving behind her final shot—'You could have been a marchioness, but you settled for being a slut!'—ringing in Evie's ears.

Had Raschid witnessed the little altercation? She presumed he had since she could feel the heat of his anger even from here.

She only hoped he didn't decide to come over here in a gesture of support. It would only make everything ten times worse if he did. But Great-Aunt Celia's cutting demolition of her character had left its mark, and she was glad of her wide-brimmed hat because at least it was hiding the pained flush that was colouring her cheeks.

Fortunately the wedding party came back into view then, and the whole congregation rose to applaud them as the newly married couple walked down the aisle with bright beaming smiles on their happy faces.

Evie clapped with the rest of them, tears of genuine heart-warming emotion blinding her eyes. So it wasn't until the whole wedding entourage were out in the sunshine and everyone else began filing out after them that she realised someone had come to stand right behind her.

Tilting her head back so she could see who it was over the brim of her hat, she found herself looking through a bank of moisture into the lean dark face of Sheikh Raschid Al Kadah. And her heart turned over.

He was smiling down at her, the wonderful shape of his sensual mouth tilted wryly at one corner. But his eyes were sombre, their warm, dark liquid-gold depths burning with a grave kind of understanding that had her sighing as she tilted her head forward again to watch the final few stragglers drift away.

'You look beautiful,' he murmured to her gently. 'But inconsolably sad.'

'I think I want to run away and never be found again,' she confided. 'Do you think my mother may notice if I did?'

'No,' he honestly replied. 'But I would.'

Despite her heavy mood, a smile tilted the corners of her red-painted mouth. 'That's because you fancy the hell out of me,' she countered. 'Whereas my mother doesn't fancy me at all—especially as a daughter.'

'Then she has no taste.'

'Gosh,' Evie gasped. 'I wonder if she knows that?'

'Would you like me to tell her?' he kindly offered.

'No. What I would like you to do, Sheikh Raschid,' she sighed out wistfully, 'is gather me up on your white charger and take me away from all of this.'

'Right now?' A pair of long-fingered, beautifully shaped brown hands slid around her narrow waist to turn her to face him. His eyes were still sombre despite the light banter they were exchanging. 'Just say the word, and I will carry you off to my palace in the desert and keep you locked away there for ever.'

'A fate worse than death,' she pouted. 'You have horrible dungeons there with no windows to look out of. I know,' she disclosed sagely. 'Because you told me.'

'I have beautiful rooms too,' he declared. 'Which overlook exquisite gardens that cost me an absolute fortune to irrigate. You may have one of those rooms,' he offered benevolently. 'Where I will visit you every day to ply you with priceless gifts and incomparable compliments.'

'May I move around your desert palace freely?' she asked.

He shook his covered head. 'You will be my prisoner,' he explained. 'With guards posted at the door to make sure you don't stray.'

'What if I fancy one of your guards for a bit of light diversion?'

'They would all be eunuchs,' he came back blandly. 'The kind of light diversion you are referring to will make them of no use to you.'

'I don't want to go, then,' Evie decided. 'I'll be more miserable there than I am here.'

'That's my girl,' Raschid softly commended, drawing her even closer to that lean, tight body hiding behind the flowing robes. 'Counting your blessings is always the wiser course in situations like these.'

She laughed. He smiled, the smile reaching his eyes now that he had managed to banish the sadness from hers. And, dipping his head beneath the brim of her hat, he kissed her.

They were by now completely alone beneath the wedding canopy, so Evie didn't really need to pull away quite as quickly as she did. Their mouths had barely warmed in welcome to each other before she was carefully separating them and placing some much needed distance between their clinging bodies.

'Are you trying to seduce me in broad daylight, Sheikh?' she demanded mock sternly in an attempt to soften her rejection of him.

But Raschid refused to play the game. 'No,' he said quietly. 'I was trying to demonstrate how deeply I care for you.'

'What—here?' Evie mocked that also, but this time the mockery was ever so slightly spiked. 'In front of a Christian altar—what will your God say? Or did the tent above your head make you forget where you were for a moment?'

'My God is the same God as your God, Evie,' he answered very grimly.

'Well, just in case you're wrong, I'm off, before we get struck down by a bolt of lightning or something,' she said, clinging to her bantering tone despite his much—much graver one. 'I'll see you later—'

'Evie.'

She had already turned her back on him when he said her name like that, making her go still as the muscles around her heart gave a painful pinch.

Raschid wasn't stupid, she knew that. Those all-seeing liquid-gold eyes of his had caught the haunted look in her own eyes before she'd turned away.

'What?' she prompted warily.

There was a moment's complete silence from behind her that trickled down her rigid spine like a warning. And she closed her eyes, mouth gone dry, heart still pinching in protest at what she was struggling to keep bottled up inside her today.

'What's wrong?'

'Nothing,' she denied.

'The same "nothing" that has made you as elusive as a rare butterfly for the last few weeks?' he grimly suggested.

'You've been busy. I've been busy,' she murmured defensively.

'You've been hiding,' he corrected. 'And you are still hiding.'

'I just need to get through this day with my dignity intact, that's all,' she sighed.

'And you think that my kissing you here diminishes that dignity?' He sounded cold all of a sudden—as haughty as hell. Which was a bad sign. For Raschid a bruised ego always—always made him insufferably arrogant.

'I did warn you not to come,' she reminded him.

'And because I refuse to hide like you I am to be punished, is that it?'

Put like that, he had a right to sound offended, Evie wearily acknowledged. 'You're a man,' she said dryly. 'Bedding one of England's most eligible females only adds to your standing, whereas I get called a cheap little slut.'

'The woman in the awful lilac dress!' Raschid recognised instantly. 'The words match her sour expression.'

Despite her heavy mood, Evie couldn't resist smiling at his caustic description of dear Great-Aunt Celia. 'To be fair,' she twisted around to say to him, 'she did call you a womanising barbarian.'

A sleek, superbly drawn black eyebrow arched in enquiry. 'And you agree with her?'

'Oh, yes,' she admitted. 'But then,' she added softly, 'I like you barbaric.'

The darkening look in his eyes set her stomach fluttering.

'I have to go,' she murmured, turning away what that fluttering sensation was tempting.

'More evasion?'

'I'll see you later,' was all she replied, and walked gracefully away.

Stepping out from beneath the sultry-aired canopy was like stepping into another world. The sun was bright, the air crystal-clear, and the sights and sounds of celebration were everywhere.

The bridal party was posing for photographers in front of a perfectly placed beech tree that looked as if it had been standing there for at least a thousand years. All about them their guests stood around in small groups watching them. A small army of white-jacketed waiters wove in and out with silver trays laden with fluted champagne glasses, trying to avoid the children who were running about like swirling dervishes and letting off steam.

The band was still playing, and it seemed odd to Evie that she hadn't heard a single note while she had been with Raschid.

But then, Raschid had that kind of effect on her. When he was there her world began and ended with him alone. Which was why this other world out here felt so very strange and alien.

Julian caught sight of her and called out, then waved his hand in an imperious command for her to come and join them. Evie nodded her head in acknowledgement but took her time making her way over there. Her brother didn't know it, but she had no intention of appearing with them on any photograph.

So she stopped a waiter to collect a champagne glass, paused then to chat lightly to the first group of people she came to. Saw, from the corner of her eye, her brother's attention become claimed by more pressing duties that made him forget all about her, and kept her social smile fixed firmly in place as she wandered from group to group—the only group she carefully avoided being the Arab contingent.

Someone appeared at her shoulder and tentatively touched her arm. She turned her head, the social smile still fixed firmly in place, found herself looking into the rue-fully smiling face of an attractive man with brown hair, grey eyes and a shy disposition.

And instantly her expression mellowed into true tenderness. 'Harry,' she greeted softly. 'How lovely to see you.' It was purely instinctive for her to go up on tiptoe to press a kiss to his lean cheek.

From not very far away several people stood observing the exchange from completely different perspectives. Her mother observed with unmasked satisfaction, Raschid with grim speculation as he watched Evie's face, saw that smile as the one he'd always believed was reserved exclusively for him—and discovered that it hit him rather hard to know another man warranted such tenderness.

He knew, of course, who the guy was, and what he had once been to Evie. They had been childhood friends, sweethearts in their teenage years—but never lovers, he reminded himself as he watched the Marquis of Lister place hands that most definitely coveted around Evie's slender waist.

'He's still in love with her,' a cold voice murmured beside him. 'She broke his heart when she left him for you. Will you break her heart, Sheikh Raschid, when it's time for you to let my daughter go?'

'I wonder what appeals to you more, Lady Delahaye,' Raschid smiled tightly. 'The prospect of your daughter receiving that broken heart or my leaving her?'

'I love Evie,' Evie's mother declared stiffly.

'Really?' he drawled. 'Then I beg leave to inform you that it doesn't show.'

'She has a right to be able to stand alongside the man she loves with her head held high in pride, not to avoid his presence at all cost!'

'And whose fault is it that she does avoid me?' Raschid challenged. 'Certainly not mine,' he denied.

'She doesn't look well,' Evie's mother stated tightly. 'She most certainly doesn't look happy. And that smile she is offering Harry is the first genuine smile I've seen from her today.'

'I know...' Raschid acknowledged quietly, his mind locked on something else Lady Delahaye had said that had managed to strike at the very heart of him.

Because, he realised, Evie didn't look well. He knew

she was unhappy—that much had been patently obvious to him for several weeks now.

But ill—as in sick? A chill went whipping though him.

'Excuse me,' he said curtly, and walked away, leaving Lucinda Delahaye to follow his long, lean, graceful approach towards her daughter with angrily resentful eyes.

Resentment that turned to grim satisfaction when she saw her son and his new bride waylay Sheikh Raschid before he could reach his target. She could see his frustration behind the smile of congratulation he had fixed on his lean dark face. And she could see Evie, so engrossed in whatever Harry was saying to her that she wasn't aware that her lover stood not ten feet away.

Thank goodness for Julian, Evie was thinking as she pretended to listen to Harry enthuse about the innovative breeding programme he was using at his racing stud, while her real attention was fixed on Raschid, and the disturbing fact that he had been striding purposefully towards her.

She'd seen her mother speak to him, seen by both their expressions that the short meeting had not broken any ice. Whatever her mother had said to Raschid it had made him excuse himself curtly and make directly for Evie, which could only mean one thing.

Her mother was stirring trouble.

'You should come down some time and see what we're doing there,' Harry was saying. 'You won't believe the changes since you last visited, Evie.'

Laughter suddenly exploded into the afternoon air, Julian and Raschid sounding deep and hearty, Christina's lighter laughter like the tinkling of fairy bells, sweet and delicate and undeniably happy.

And once again Evie was glad of her wide-brimmed gauzy hat that was hiding her envious wish to be with them instead of standing here with Harry.

Harry, whom she had once thought she loved to distraction but now couldn't even remember what that love felt like since it had been so thoroughly overwhelmed by what she felt for Raschid.

'But your mother tells me you don't get down to Westhaven much any more.' Harry's voice reached out to her from what felt like a long, long way off. 'Is that because you didn't fancy running into me?'

'What?' Dragging her attention away from the laughing trio, Evie made her eyes focus on Harry's uncomfortably flushed face. 'Don't be an idiot, Harry,' she admonished. 'We were very good friends once. I thought we still were.'

'I embarrassed you by asking you to marry me.' He grimaced.

'I was very honoured that you asked me,' Evie replied. 'And very sad that I had to turn you down. But it wouldn't have worked for you and me, Harry,' she added softly, watching the way his restless grey eyes couldn't look directly at her. 'We knew each other too well, were too— comfortable with each other.'

'There were no exciting sparks flying between us, you mean.' He laughed tensely. 'Not the sort that fly between you and your Sheikh, anyway.'

There was no kind way to answer that, so Evie didn't offer one. Instead she turned the conversation back to the safer ground of horses. Not long after that, the Master of Ceremonies called for them to take their places in the main marquee where the wedding banquet was to be served.

Seating four hundred guests around huge round tables was no small feat, and for the next couple of hours Evie didn't so much as lay eyes on Raschid, her place being with family relatives and his amongst the dignitaries seated right over on the other side of the marquee.

So the day crawled on, through course after course of delicately prepared dishes and benign conversation. The speeches began, the champagne glasses being constantly refilled to mark each toast offered to the bride and groom.

By the time people began to drift away to go and get

ready for the ball that evening, Evie was beginning to feel very jaded. She went to her room and indulged herself in a long soak in the antiquated cast-iron bath in the vague hope it would help remove some of the tension from her body.

It didn't. So the knock at her bedroom door as she was just pulling a satin robe over the flesh-coloured teddy she intended to wear beneath the gold dress tonight made her heart sink in weary anticipation of yet another lecture from her mother as she called a very reluctant, 'Come in!'

And was therefore surprised when it was Raschid who stepped into the room.

# CHAPTER FOUR

HER horror must have shown on her face, because his expression was not a pleasant one as he firmly shut the door behind him and pointedly twisted the key in the lock. Then he was turning to lean his broad shoulders back against the solid oak and folding his arms across his chest in what she could only describe as his confrontational pose.

Gone were the flowing white robes of the Arab and in their place were the clothes of the super-sophisticated western man. White shirt, black bow tie, creamy white dinner jacket and black silk trousers that accentuated the length of his powerfully muscled legs.

Evie's insides began to flutter, her eyes darkening warily as she made herself look into the grimness of his. He was glancing around the room with an expression of unconcealed disfavour.

'Your brother was not exaggerating when he informed his lovely new wife that you had been insulted,' he remarked. 'It is no wonder her cheeks flushed with mortification as she went off to take the issue up with her mother, who then flushed and blamed your own mother—who had apparently...' his hard eyes flicked to Evie '...made a special request that you be accommodated as far away from the west wing of the castle as they could possibly place you...'

The west wing being where Raschid would be accommodated—in one of the very large and very grand bedroom suites, Evie assumed. And was unable to hide the hurt she experienced on learning that her own mother could be so petty in her disapproval of her relationship with Raschid that she could go to such extremes.

'Just say the word,' Raschid said coolly, 'and I will have your things moved in with mine.'

'I'm fine where I am,' she said, wondering if her mother truly believed she could prove a point with such action. Did she honestly think it would keep them apart if they had no wish to be apart?

Half a mile of draughty corridor was certainly no deterrent to Raschid, anyway.

'Is that why you're here?' she asked a trifle wearily. 'To check out my supposedly insulting accommodation?'

'No...' His dark head shook, those golden eyes of his grimly fixed on her tired face. 'I am here to enquire after your health.'

'My health?' Evie frowned at him in puzzled confusion. 'Was that your sweet way of being sarcastic?'

'No,' he denied. 'I was being sincere. To put it bluntly, Evangeline,' he added, using her full name in much the same way her mother did—as a warning of worse to come, 'you look wretched.'

Oh, great, she thought. 'I'm fine,' she said, turning away from those too shrewd golden eyes.

'Pale and pathetic,' he went on as if she hadn't spoken. 'Too frail to stand up and too tense to sit down.'

'I said,' Evie flashed at him in irritation, 'I feel fine! There is absolutely nothing wrong with me!'

The simple fact that she was snapping at him was telling Raschid the opposite. His eyes narrowed, the aggressive stance he had taken up against the door altering to one of dangerous challenge.

'Good,' he murmured. 'Then you can have no objection to my escorting you down to the ballroom, can you?' he tagged on very silkily.

Evie sighed, wishing that this day were already over and done with. 'Raschid—' she began wearily.

'Raschid—nothing,' he coolly cut in. 'I have played my

official role here today, to perfection. So have you. Now it is time to relax and begin enjoying ourselves.'

Relax—nothing. Evie parodied him inside her head. He was angry with her for avoiding him all afternoon and he was here to fight, not enjoy himself.

'Do you have a problem with that?' he enquired when she didn't say anything.

'Several,' Evie answered dryly. 'But I don't think you're in any mood to hear them.'

'Wise girl,' he commended. 'Now be even wiser, and slip your delectable body into whatever it is you are wearing tonight before I decide that it may be more satisfying to toss you down on that excuse for a bed behind you and assuage my anger in other ways.'

'Novel,' she mocked, feeling some rather well known but unwanted sensations go chasing through her system at the prospect of his alternative. 'But I am not walking out of this room with you, Raschid, with my mother standing guard only a few doors away. She would have my guts for garters.'

'And I will have them for a noose which I will tie around your beautiful neck if you don't walk out with me,' he countered. 'So, which will it be, Evie? Your mother's pride or my pride? Take your pick.'

The direct challenge.

Evie sighed one of those sighs she'd caught herself doing a lot recently, and went to drop down on her dressing stool. 'Don't do this to me tonight, Raschid,' she pleaded heavily. 'I've got a headache and I'm really not up to it.'

'I know the feeling,' he grimly commiserated. 'In fact, I am thoroughly annoyed with both you and your prejudiced family,' he clipped out. 'To the extent that if I am provoked any further today I may just disgrace myself by telling them all what I think of them!'

'And that includes telling me, it seems.' Despite his anger and her own depression, Evie found a rueful smile from somewhere.

'Quite,' he clipped. 'So be sensible, Evie, and humour me unless you want to see an ugly scene erupt in the Beverley ballroom.'

He meant it too; Evie could see that in the grim cut of his mouth as he levered himself away from the door and walked across the room to the antiquated wardrobe, much as her mother had done several hours ago.

Only, the similarity ended with the opening of the wardrobe door. For Raschid took one look at the dress hanging there—and began to chuckle. 'I knew you were brave,' he grinned. 'But not this brave.'

'Brazen is the word my great-aunt Celia used,' Evie informed him.

Turning with the dress over his arm, he laid it on the bed then came over to where she was sitting.

'Up,' he said firmly, curving long fingers around her upper arms to help her.

Then, because she looked so adorably pathetic with that miserable expression on her face, he bent his dark head and kissed her—and when all she did was sigh shakily into his mouth he deepened the kiss until the sighing stopped and she began clinging.

'Now…' he said when he eventually drew away again. 'Do you dress yourself or do I do it for you?'

'I don't suppose you would consider letting me get through the rest of today in my own way?' she suggested hopefully.

The dark head shook, his hands already dealing with the knotted belt around her waist.

'Mmm,' he murmured, when her robe fell open to reveal a flesh-coloured silk teddy that hardly hid what it was supposed to be covering. 'Very seductive.'

Long, knowing fingers made a caressing journey from her tiny waist to the proud thrust of her breasts. His thumb pads teased her with little passes across the tight nubs of her nipples and a different kind of sigh escaped her, one that whimpered like an anxious kitten while her slender hips writhed as those teasing caresses made other parts of her stir into sweet, throbbing life.

'I've missed that little sigh,' Raschid whispered softly, his eyes possessive on her as he watched her sink into that sensual trance his touch always induced. 'I've missed you,' he added huskily.

'I can tell,' she sighed out pleasurably. He was very aroused—but then, so was she. They had not been together like this for two weeks now—a long time for them. 'Kiss me,' she groaned.

He responded quickly, hotly, hungrily, his mouth covering hers with a driving force that had her head snapping back on a slender neck while his arms crushed her tightly to him.

He was alive and wanting, his mouth urgent now as it kissed and sucked and licked and tasted its way across her cheek and jaw while his hands moved lower again, cupping her around her silky thighs before his fingers slid beneath the teddy and drew her hard up against him.

'Raschid—' she groaned as he set his hips moving against her in an age-old rhythm that set an equally old rhythm pulsing inside herself. 'We haven't got time for this.'

'I can be quick,' he murmured audaciously. 'Five minutes and you will feel wonderful, I promise you...'

'Incorrigible man,' she scolded, then gasped when knowing fingers slid along her buttocks until they reached what they were searching for.

She was warm and she was moist and she was ready for him. She never could put up much of a resistance to him. Her hands jerked up, clutching at his arms for support as he captured her mouth with a kiss that tossed her into a world of frantic hunger.

'Release me,' Raschid pleaded hoarsely against her mouth.

Fingers trembling in their urgency, she did as he bade her, drawing down the zip on his evening trousers and releasing him from the silk shorts he wore beneath. He filled her hand, hard and throbbing, smooth as silk, such a potent source of power and pleasure that her control went haywire. It didn't matter—not when it was so apparent that his control was no better. His heart was pounding, his breathing shot. Two red streaks across his lean dark cheekbones were underlining the ruthless intent burning in his eyes as he edged her backwards until the backs of her thighs met with the edge of the solid oak dressing table.

With a fierce sexual urgency he parted her white thighs and pressed his own taut brown ones between them. Then, with the deftness of experience, he released her lower body from the silk teddy and bent his knees so he could enter her cleanly.

His grunt of satisfaction as he felt her muscles close greedily around him was matched by her groan of pleasure. Her fingers were clutching his neck, her spine arching over his supporting arm so he could suck on her breasts through the teddy while he drove them both to a place beyond bearing.

And he was right. Five minutes later and she did feel wonderful, limp and languid, not a hint of tension or stress in her.

'Now you look less like a haunted woman,' he murmured softly, golden eyes darkened to polished bronze by sensual satisfaction as they viewed her.

'And you look ridiculous with your trousers round your shoes,' Evie countered tauntingly.

But he just grinned, all slashing white teeth and pure male arrogance. Even in a situation like this, Raschid knew he looked devastatingly sexy. He was still inside her, his hands holding her against the cradle of his lean hips while his eyes ran tenderly over her love-softened face.

'I adore you, you know...' he softly informed her. 'If the world stopped turning at this precise moment, I could die a happy man.'

Evie almost told him then. Almost... Almost tested that statement with words that would surely make his world stand still. But—

No.

The need to get through what was left of today without causing a major disaster was paramount. So, 'Your five minutes are up,' she said, and felt his soft laugh vibrate in the very essence of her before he ruefully and reluctantly drew away.

He helped her to dress, smoothly drawing up the zip on the gold silk gown then standing back to watch her with darkly possessive eyes as she twisted up her hair, then sat down to replenish her make-up.

Getting up to slip her feet into the strappy gold shoes, Evie then turned towards him to announce she was ready. Seeing a question written in his love-sated eyes, she smiled her answer.

No more compromising for the sake of her mother. They would go down to the ball together and damn the consequences.

For this could be the last time she would be able to show herself in public with him like this.

Julian and Christina were dancing the first waltz when they entered the ballroom. The lights had been dimmed, and a single spotlight followed the bride and groom around while everyone was standing around the dance floor, thankfully too busy clapping and teasing the newly-weds to notice Evie and Raschid's arrival.

With her hand resting in the crook of Raschid's arm, Evie watched from the sidelines as gradually other couples began to join the newly-weds. Lord Beverley with his wife, Robert Malvern gallantly inviting Evie's mother to dance.

'Shall we?' Raschid murmured.

'Why not?' she replied, but there was a lot of bravado in her tone and he arched his sleek black eyebrows at her as he drew her into his arms then danced off with a lightness of foot that secretly made her breathless.

'You're good at this,' she remarked, keeping her eyes fixed on his face so she didn't have to see the kind of looks they would be receiving.

'It is expected of a dashing Arab prince,' he blandly mocked himself. 'I can jive too, and I'm not bad at the Gay Gordon.'

'You don't have a modest bone in your body, either,' Evie tagged on dryly.

'Thank you.' Arrogant as always, he took the remark as a compliment. 'Of course, a lack of modesty forces me to say that I am also dancing with the most beautiful woman in the room.'

Her mother danced close by, and Evie stiffened slightly at the glowering look she received. 'Stop it,' Raschid admonished. 'Or I will take you back upstairs again.'

'Fate worse than death,' she quipped.

'So you found her, Raschid.'

Julian and Christina swished up beside them. Christina looked radiant, her gentle eyes sparkling.

'As you directed,' Raschid replied. 'I turned to the east and walked on to the end of the earth.'

Immediately the spark went out of Christina's eyes. 'I'm so sorry about your room, Evie,' she cried in mortification. 'I didn't know until Julian told me!'

'Don't be silly, the room is fine!' Evie assured her.

'And maybe she deserved it after all,' her brother put in. 'Since she couldn't even bring herself to appear in one small photograph with us!'

Raschid's eyes narrowed. Evie's cheeks flushed. The information was obviously new to him. 'Why not?' he demanded.

'Because she didn't like the company,' Julian suggested tauntingly.

'Don't be cruel, Ju,' his new bride scolded him. 'You know why Evie did it!'

'Then perhaps you would like to explain it to me, Christina,' Raschid drawled. 'Excuse me, Julian, for I am about to steal your bride for a little while...'

And as deftly as that Raschid swapped partners, and was dancing off with a blushing bride clinging to his tall, lean, elegant frame, leaving sister and brother staring ruefully after them.

'I think he's angry,' Julian remarked.

'That makes two of you, obviously,' his sister wearily replied.

'Three actually,' Julian said, then sighed as he tugged her into his arms and danced after the other two. 'Mother came by your room earlier,' he told her.

'What?' Appalled, Evie's voice left her throat as a half-hysterical squeak. 'I hope you're teasing me, Julian!' she gasped out shakily.

'Why, what were you doing?' he asked. Then grinned a typically rakish male grin when Evie blushed from breast to hairline. 'Oh, wow. No wonder she's on the warpath again,' he said. 'I hope you had the sense to lock the door...'

'Raschid did,' she mumbled.

'Good old Raschid,' her brother mocked. 'Always thinking ahead of himself, that guy.'

'She didn't actually say she heard us, did she?' Evie asked anxiously.

Looking down at her with wickedly teasing eyes, Julian drew out the silence while he pondered whether or not to lie—then laughed out loud as his poor sister's face went from blush-red to paste-white. 'She heard the two of you talking, that's all.' He finally let Evie off the hook.

'I think I hate you,' she choked, her chest feeling as if it had just collapsed.

'Punishment,' he said unsympathetically. 'For being so pathetic as to believe your absence from my wedding photos is going to stop the gossip columnists from marking yours and Raschid's presence here. What they will do,' he went on grimly, 'is make a whole lot of mischief out of the way you carefully avoided him. Intrigue,' he incised, 'is the spice of their lives, Evie. And you certainly gave them enough spice to make a meal out of your behaviour today.'

'I didn't want them splashing photos of me and him all over their papers instead of you and Christina,' she defended herself.

'Well, having thwarted them of a photograph, they will instead make much of the fact that they couldn't catch the two of you together—anywhere. And how do I know that?' he concluded. 'Because those were the kind of questions most of our guests were pumped with today by the reporters. Which in turn made your entrance here tonight on Raschid's arm a real revelation—for everyone.'

'You noticed?'

'You are such a naïve little baby sometimes, Evie,' her brother sighed. Standing several inches taller than her, Julian dropped his gaze to her surprised face. 'I would think that the whole room noticed—which was why Raschid did it, isn't it?' he suggested. 'He'd had enough of playing the nasty skeleton in your dark little cupboard. The man has more than his fair share of pride, and you kicked it today with your behaviour.'

By the time Raschid came back to graciously return the bride to her new husband, Evie was trying to come to terms with the unpalatable fact that she seemed to have upset just about everyone she cared about today, in one way or another.

He didn't speak as he danced her away again, but the fingers that held her were saying a lot and he was wearing that cold, hard mask on his face that she knew very well.

'I did warn you,' she said, unable to say nothing even when expediency was telling her that silence in this case was the better part of valour.

'So you did,' he agreed. 'It is a shame there were no hidden cameras in your bedroom earlier, for we could have stopped the gossips in their curious tracks then.'

'Oh, don't be such a boor, Raschid,' Evie flashed, guilty conscience giving way to anger. 'Tell me,' she demanded. 'What would you have done if our roles here had been reversed, and this had been Ranya's wedding day, to which, by some utterly amazing quirk of fate, I had been invited?'

The smooth line of his jaw clenched, the angry outline of his mouth tightening even further as he took the very sarcastic scenario on board.

'You would have asked me not to attend the wedding.' She gave the answer for him. 'And if, like you, I had told you to go to hell, you would then have made a point of completely ignoring me! But—unlike you,' she then added tightly, 'I would have accepted your desire for privacy, hurt though I may have been by it. The word is dignity, Raschid,' she clipped at him coldly. 'Something you should recognise since you have so much of it. Well, today I was protecting my dignity, not yours. And if you don't like that, then it's just too damned bad!'

It was fortunate, perhaps, that the music finished then. Evie flashed his ice-cold mask of a face one final searing glance then walked angrily away. But the sense of tight hurt she experienced as she did so was there because he let her do it.

After that, she went back to avoiding him—as she did

anyone who might think it was their right to castigate her for one sin or another! Instead she stuck to those people who couldn't care less what she did in her private life. She laughed, she danced, she chatted and teased and generally sparkled like a golden icon to beauty and social charm.

While inside she had never felt so lonely in her entire life.

The time came at last for the bride and groom to depart and everyone gathered in the castle's great hallway to see them off. They were staying at one of the hotels close to Heathrow tonight before flying off to Barbados first thing in the morning.

Christina appeared at the top of the grand staircase dressed in a blush-pink Dior suit. In her hands she carried her wedding bouquet, and behind her Julian was grinning as he listened to the calls for his bride to throw the lucky flowers.

Evie stood and teased and called with the rest of them, but it was only the sudden flash from Christina's eyes that warned her what was coming—as the bouquet came spiralling through the air and landed against her chest.

If silence could be measured in decibels, then the sudden silence that encompassed the great hall at Beverley Castle hit whole new levels. Everyone just stood there and gaped at Evie. No teasing, no jokes. They simply did not know what to say as Evie's cheeks mottled with embarrassed colour.

From the back of the hall, Raschid witnessed it all in a kind of frozen stillness, the appalling truth that every single person here knew there was no hope of Evie marrying while she stayed with him hitting him like a punch to the solar plexus.

'Well...' Evie's voice came out light and rueful. 'We can all live and dream, I suppose.'

And dutifully the crowd laughed, but nervously, tensely. For Evie it was the worst moment of her life. She kept smiling, though. With a teeth-gritting will-power she kept that darned smile in place. She hugged and kissed her brother, received a penitent Christina into her arms.

'I'm sorry, Evie,' the bride whispered. 'I didn't mean to—'

'Shh,' she cut in, and kissed Christina's cheek. 'Just go away, have a lovely honeymoon!'

By the time the car went off down the driveway, flying streamers and rattling tin cans, Evie had had enough. Seeing her mother making a beeline for her had her turning quickly in the opposite direction and slipping away into the soft summer darkness.

The lake beckoned, its moon-kissed silk-smooth surface acting like a soothing lure to her storm-tossed senses. Walking around the main marquee, she stepped up to the lake rim, and watched bleakly as the view in front of her went out of focus through eyes that slowly filled with tears.

Well, she told herself. She'd done it. She had got through today—though not quite as she'd wanted to get through it. She'd upset many and pleased none. But at least now she could concentrate on pleasing Evie.

And Evie wanted to—

Her heart began to throb. The deep dark well of frustration and misery she had been keeping such a firm hold on all day suddenly burst through its constraints. And with a fierceness that said it all she stretched out the hand still clutching Christina's bouquet and with as much power as she could muster tossed the flowers as far as she could into the lake.

The bouquet landed with a soft splash, bobbed a couple of times, then lay there floating in a pool of moon-kissed ripples.

'Feel better for that?' a dark voice said behind her.

'Not so you would notice,' she said, not bothering to turn because she knew who it was. 'Go away, Raschid,' she then added flatly. 'I don't need another round in the verbal boxing ring with you, right now.'

'No,' he murmured gravely. 'I can see that...'

She heard him move, her body tensed up as muscles tightened in screaming protest. The tears came back, so strong this time that they set her throat working and her soft mouth quivering. She closed her eyes over the tears, clamped her quivering mouth shut and clenched her hands into two tight fists at her sides while she waited for him to take the hint and leave, or ignore the hint with his usual arrogance.

The silence hummed, the tension along with it. After what felt like an age and no more sound came from behind her, Evie began slowly to relax the tension out of her body. He had shown sensitivity for once and left her alone, she assumed.

And on a long, long heavy sigh that seemed to come from the very lowest regions of her she kicked the strappy high-heeled shoes from her aching feet, released her hair from its uncomfortable knot, then lowered herself on to the bone-dry short-shorn grass to sit staring out at the glassy still lake.

In a little while, she told herself, she would go back into the castle and creep away to her room. Then tomorrow—

Another sigh. Tomorrow was just another day fraught with a different set of pressing problems. Tomorrow would be deal with mother time, deal with Raschid time.

Somewhere in the darkness an owl began hooting, sounding bleak and lonely as if it was calling hopelessly for a mate. A fish rose to the water's surface, its tail making a lazy flapping noise as it rolled over, setting the bouquet of flowers bobbing again in the ripples it left behind.

She really shouldn't have done that, Evie mused guiltily. Christina would be so hurt to know that her lovely bouquet had finished up in such a watery grave.

She shivered, and her knees came up, her arms wrapping

round them, her loosened hair sliding in a thick silk curtain around her slender shoulders as she lowered her weary brow to rest it against her knees.

The feel of a jacket dropping across her hunched shoulders should have surprised her, but oddly it didn't. She would have been more surprised if Raschid had simply walked away and left her to it.

'I thought you'd gone,' she said.

'No,' was all he replied, and dropped down on the grass beside her.

Turning her face on her knees so she could look at him through the curtain of her hair, Evie found herself gazing at a sombre profile that was, even so, the most beautifully structured profile she had ever seen. Like her, his knees were up, but parted so his wrists could rest upon them. His dress shirt stood out bright in the moonlight; his skin was like polished bronze.

Her heart swelled in her breast, swelled and swelled until she thought it was going to burst under the power of her wretched love for him.

He turned to look at her, sombre-eyed and flat-mouthed. 'Are you ready to tell me what is wrong, now?'

No, she thought miserably. I'm not ready. I'll never be ready. And she turned her face to stare moodily at the lake so she didn't have to look at him.

'Your mother thinks you are ill,' he added when it became obvious that she wasn't going to say anything.

I am, she thought. Soul-sick and heartbroken. 'I didn't know you had that kind of conversation with my mother,' she remarked.

'I don't, usually,' he dryly admitted. 'But this one took the form of a—confrontation.'

Ah, Evie was very intimate with *those* kinds of conversations with her mother. 'I'm not ill,' she assured him.

'Then what the hell is the matter with you?' he rasped,

suddenly losing all patience. 'Because it has been patently obvious to me for weeks now that something certainly is!'

'I thought I told you I didn't want another verbal battle tonight!' she snapped right back.

'Then don't turn this into one!' He turned the tables on her as quick as a flash. 'You are my life, my heart, my soul, Evie,' he added gruffly. 'I would do anything for you; I thought you knew that.'

'Except marry me,' she said, then grimaced at herself for stupidly blurting it out like that.

His answering sigh was heavy. It wasn't words but— good grief—it spoke volumes in other ways. 'Is that what this is all about?'

'No,' she denied, and went to get up, but his hand came out to press her down again.

'Talk,' he commanded. 'Or reconcile yourself to the uncomfortable prospect of spending the night right here.'

He meant it, too; that tough macho gleam was in his eyes again. On a sigh she subsided. He let go of her, recognising the sigh as a gesture of defeat. Evie turned her gaze back to the moonlit lake once again, felt a tightness pull around her chest, and said flatly, 'I'm pregnant.'

## CHAPTER FIVE

As ANNOUNCEMENTS went, this one truly took the trophy. To his credit, Raschid didn't groan in horror or curse and shout, or demand to know how the hell she had allowed such a stupid thing to happen. All the things he certainly had a right to do.

In fact, he didn't do anything. He just continued to sit there, as silent as death, as still as stone, utilising that impressive bank of self-discipline Evie knew he possessed to hold himself in check while he attempted to take the shocking news in.

And it was awful—worse, much worse than she'd even envisaged this moment was going to be because she knew this man so very well, and knowing him meant she understood exactly what his silence was actually saying.

Raschid's world and all it meant to him had just been effectively brought tumbling down around him. And this was more than just the noble Arab prince holding his emotions in check as he had been trained from birth to do in times of disaster.

He was sitting there like that because he was literally paralysed with dismay.

'Say something,' she prompted when she could stand his silence no longer.

'Like what?' he asked, then admitted grimacingly, 'I find I am struck speechless.'

Well, speechless just about covered it, Evie thought painfully. 'How, where and when seem good places to start,' she huskily suggested.

'Okay…' At last he moved, turning his head to look at

her—though Evie couldn't bring herself to look back at him now.

'How?' He began with her first suggestion.

Her hunched shoulders gave a helpless shrug. 'I don't know how,' she answered honestly. 'Somewhere along the line, my birth control has let me down but I just don't know how it did. The where depends on the when,' she went on huskily. 'Which was about six weeks ago,' she calculated. 'Which in turn probably means it happened during the weekend we spent together on your yacht in the Mediterranean,' she assumed. 'Though I will know better when I see a doctor...'

'So this is not yet confirmed?'

Did he have to sound so damned hopeful? Her chest began to hurt with the tension she was putting on it, her throat locking up on a tight ball of emotion she didn't dare release.

'Home testing sets are pretty accurate these days,' she informed him flatly.

Another long silence followed that, one that throbbed and pulled and picked at the flesh like an animal chewing on a dead carcass. Only Evie's carcass wasn't dead. It was alive and hurting in more ways than she would have believed possible.

Out on the lake the owl hooted its lonely call for a mate again. The moon slithered its eerie way across the glass-smooth waters—and Christina's bouquet continued to float right there in front of them, making really heavy irony now of its good-luck significance.

'You knew about this two weeks ago, didn't you?' he said suddenly.

What was the use in lying? 'Yes,' she replied.

'Damn it, Evie!' His control suddenly exploded, launching him to his feet as shock gave way to a burst of anger. 'Why didn't you tell me then? Do you have any conception of what those two weeks are going to mean to me?' He lashed at her. 'The problems they are going to cause?' A sigh shot from him, his dark face contorting with blistering condemnation as he violently spun his back on her. 'What a mess!' he muttered thickly. 'What a damned mess!'

White-faced and shaken by his scorching response, Evie came more slowly to her feet to stand staring at him in utter dismay. For, no matter how terrible she had expected his reaction to be, she hadn't expected anything quite so brutal as this.

'What difference can two weeks possibly make to the situation?' she demanded shakily.

He didn't answer; instead a hand went up to grip the back of his angry neck, the action showing all the horror and frustration he was currently experiencing.

In fact, he couldn't have been more horrified if she'd told him she'd infected him with some dreadful social disease.

'Unless, of course, you're hoping I may offer to do something about it?' she then suggested, wanting to twist the knife she could almost see sticking out of his ribs where she had apparently plunged it.

It worked. He flinched. 'No!' he ground out, spinning round to glare at her. 'Don't *ever*,' he gritted, 'make a suggestion like that again!'

Well, at least that was something, Evie grimly acknowledged as she stood there staring into those glitter-hard golden eyes. But then, if he had said anything else—so much as glanced at her with a hopeful look in those wretched eyes—she would never have forgiven him.

As it was, Evie shuddered on a wave of sickening self-disgust for voicing such an option just because she wanted to score points off him. 'It's all right,' she said. 'It was never a choice you were going to be offered.'

'Then why say it?' he lashed at her.

Her small laugh was forced and shrill. 'You couldn't make your horror clearer if you were being faced with the end of my brother's shotgun!' She angrily derided the question.

'You expect me to be ecstatic?'

'No,' she said heavily, turning away from him to stare bleakly out across the moon-kissed lake because looking at him now hurt just too damned much. 'But a bit of tender concern at some point wouldn't have gone amiss...'

The dry remark had his chest expanding on a strained intake of air. When he let it out again most of his anger went with it. 'I'm sorry,' he apologised gruffly. 'But, as you can no doubt appreciate, it is going to take me some time to get my head around this.'

'Get your head around what exactly?' Evie drawled, withdrawing behind her own stone-cold shell of self-protection. 'The problematic mistress who has stupidly gone and got herself pregnant?'

'It takes two to make a baby,' he sighed.

'But only one to bring it safely into the world,' Evie pointed out. 'Your part is done. Mine is just starting.'

A small silence followed that remark. Then Raschid demanded, 'Are you suggesting that I ignore the fact that you are having my baby?'

Why? Evie thought bitterly. Are you offering up a suitable alternative? 'I am suggesting that you get your priorities right,' she said. 'And remember your duty.'

Raschid stood staring into cold-cut lavender-blue eyes set in an excruciatingly beautiful face that showed not a hint of emotion anywhere on it—and at last it began to hit him just what she was saying here.

'Don't be foolish!' he snapped. 'In this case my duty is to you and the child!' A long-fingered hand flicked out in a grim, tight throw-away gesture. 'We will have to get married, of course.'

Still no words of love, Evie noted painfully. Still no words of caring. But oh, so arrogant, she observed. So damned sure of himself—so utterly dismayed by what he was so magnanimously offering.

'We don't *have* to do anything,' she countered, feeling so cold inside now that she wished she hadn't let his jacket slip to the grass when she'd got to her feet earlier.

'I will have to speak to my father...' he muttered, too busy lost in his own frowning thoughts to have heard her. 'It is going to cause problems at home, but that cannot be helped now. I will...'

'Excuse me,' Evie inserted, and this time the sheer coldness of her voice managed to gain his attention. 'But the way I see it, Raschid,' she said firmly, 'you don't have a problem here. I do.'

'What the hell is that supposed to mean?' he jerked out, beginning to look just a little shell-shocked now.

'I've never expected marriage from you,' Evie informed him. 'And I am not asking you for it now.'

'Are you mad?' he choked. 'Of course you will marry me! What else can we do?'

Oh, his sensitivity knew no bounds! Evie mocked him bitterly as she bent to retrieve her discarded shoes. 'I wouldn't marry you, Sheikh Raschid Al Kadah, if you came gift-wrapped in rubies!' she hissed as she straightened up again. 'I have too much damned respect for myself, you see!'

'Are you saying that I don't respect you?'

'Do you?' Evie flashed back. 'You see, I find it hard to reconcile the fact that I wasn't fit to marry before I became pregnant with your child!'

At last those angry golden eyes began to burn with a pained understanding of what was actually going on here. Remorse tightened his arrogant features.

'Evie...' he sighed, the hand he used to capture her wrist tense with frustration. 'I have handled this badly,' he acknowledged. 'I apologise.'

'Don't bother,' Evie snapped, tugging angrily at her imprisoned wrist. 'Let go of me,' she commanded shakily.

'Not until you listen to me,' he refused. The hand pulled her closer, drawing her fully against his powerful chest. 'You cannot expect me to pretend to be pleased about a baby when you know as well as I do the kind of problems that are going to erupt around us!'

'Funny really,' she said, lifting lavender eyes turned into dark purple pools by the sudden flood of tears washing across them. 'But I expected nothing more than I got from you, Raschid. Which just about says it all, doesn't it?'

His sigh was driven, the hand he brought around her waist there to stop her from pulling against her captive wrist. 'I thought we loved each other well enough to be honest with each other.'

'There is honest and there is brutal,' Evie said thickly. 'I feel frightened. I feel vulnerable. I feel as if I've ruined both our lives. And all you can do is worry about how this is all going to affect you!'

'I'm sorry,' he sighed yet again.

But—too late, Evie thought, and pulled herself free of him.

'Listen to me,' he pleaded. 'We need— What are you doing?' he raked out in disbelief as Evie began to walk away. 'Come back here, you exasperating creature!' he growled after her. 'You cannot just walk away from this!'

Just watch me! Evie thought wretchedly. 'In the profound words of a certain arrogant swine I know,' she tossed at him over her shoulder, 'go to hell!'

Two people knocked on her bedroom door that night. Both tried the handle when they received no response. Both discovered that the door was locked.

One was her mother; Evie knew that because Lucinda had called out to her, the usual sharpness honed out of her voice by the thickness of the wood. The other was Raschid.

She knew that because he didn't call out, he just stood on the other side of that door like a silent but dark presence— and used other means to make her aware that he was there and hadn't given up on this.

Evie didn't sleep that night; she merely dozed, shifting restlessly about the lumpy old bed that had been her mother's idea of a punishment for a daughter who refused to toe the moral line.

So, what would the punishment be for conceiving an illegitimate baby? she wondered grimly. Total excommunication from the family?

And Raschid, she moved on to consider with the same sense of wretched derision. Did he really expect her to be grateful for his belated and very reluctant offer of marriage?

And don't forget the ever-vigilant press, Evie reminded herself as she lay there in the darkness. They were going to make a real meal out of all of this if or when they ever found out about it. And neither excommunication nor marriage was going to stop their acid pens from writing their poison.

Maybe the other option was the better one. Maybe a quick if bloody end to this was the only way to save everyone's embarrassment. But even as the thought popped into her head Evie dismissed it with a telling shudder. She was whole, she was healthy, and she had no excuse—moral or otherwise—to put an end to a life before it had barely started.

And this little life had been conceived with love, even if that love now lay floundering somewhere between here and the Beverleys' private lake. She loved this baby. She loved where he came from and who he was going to be. She wanted to be there to watch him become that person. And, no matter what his father, grandmother or even his grandfather thought about it, she would make sure her child grew up feeling pride in his mixed heritage, she vowed fiercely.

By dawn she'd had enough of lying there trying to sleep when it was clear that sleep was a million miles away. Getting up, she showered in the antiquated bathroom, pulled on fresh underwear, a pair of jeans and a white tee shirt. Brushing her hair back into a simple ponytail, she then pushed her feet into lightweight slip-ons, and quietly let herself out of her room with the intention of going for a long walk before she had to face Raschid again.

There was no one about as she walked down the stairs. The hour was too early for most people after last night's partying, so she wasn't particularly surprised about that. But the house had been carefully locked up for the night, she realised belatedly, and the huge cast-iron bolts that were still rammed across the double front doors looked lethal, much too big for her to attempt to shift them.

Luckily a servant appeared in the hallway. He looked a trifle disconcerted when he saw Evie standing there so early. But he recovered quickly.

'Good morning, Miss Delahaye,' he greeted politely. 'If you're looking for the breakfast room, it's this way…'

'No—' He was about to move off when Evie stopped him. 'I was hoping to go outside for some fresh air before breakfast, but the bolts on that door look pretty much beyond me,' she explained with a rueful glance at the door.

He smiled back, half relieved he wasn't going to have to serve her yet, and came quickly towards her. Two minutes later the front door stood open, and Evie was stepping out into one of the soft, still, slightly misty mornings that were so typical of an English summer.

About to walk off to the right with the intention of making for the lake, she was stalled by the sound of a car coming up the driveway that skirted the lake on its left-hand side. A moment later the car appeared around the side of the chapel, where it stopped and the driver got out.

He saw her, and waved. It was Harry. 'Morning, Evie,' he called out, striding briskly towards her. 'You're an early bird!'

'So are you.' She found a tight smile from somewhere.

'Force of habit in my business.' He grimaced.

'But—didn't you stay here last night?' Evie asked frowningly.

He shook his head. 'I bunked down with some friends a couple of miles away,' he told her. 'But I left my jacket here last night, so I decided to collect it on my way home.'

'You're going home?' Evie's heart stopped beating for a moment, a sudden, very cowardly idea popping into her head. Harry lived only ten miles outside London.

'I have a mare due to foal at any minute,' he nodded. 'It will be her first, so I want to be there just in case there are any problems.'

'Harry—can you give me a lift home?' she asked, suddenly very sure it was what she desperately needed to do. Get away—escape.

'Of course,' he agreed, frowning slightly when he noticed belatedly the bruises around her eyes and the strained pallor of her skin.

'Can you wait while I throw my things into my bag?' Evie was already turning eagerly back to the house. 'Five minutes, Harry. I just need five minutes.'

But she was back down the stairs in only three, looking flushed rather than pale now and ever so slightly hunted as she came towards Harry who was waiting by the door with his recovered dinner jacket draped over one arm.

'Is everything all right, Evie?' he asked worriedly.

She nodded, allowing him to take her bag from her. 'It's all right,' she assured him. 'I left a note in my room for my mother, explaining where I've gone.'

'And Sheikh Raschid?'

Evie didn't answer; instead she walked out of the house

again, head down, back straight, the tension apparent in her slender frame enough to snap wire cables.

She was already sitting in the front passenger seat by the time he'd stashed away her things then climbed in beside her. Wisely holding his own counsel, Harry started the engine and turned them around. Neither spoke until they had put several long miles between them and Beverley Castle.

Then, 'Thank you,' Evie whispered.

Harry sent her a concerned glance. He had known her for most of her life, so he recognised distress when she was suffering it. 'Would you like to talk about it?' he asked.

'It's over between Raschid and I,' she heard herself announce, and wondered how she was able to say the words without breaking up inside.

But what was worse was that Harry was painfully unsurprised by the announcement. 'The rumours about it were rife last night,' he nodded. 'Something to do with his father being ill and him having to go home and marry before he can officially take over from the old man...'

For a space of thirty long, dreadful seconds, Evie didn't move—didn't breathe—didn't function on any basic level. Harry's words simply hung there in block letters in front of her while other words uttered in the heat of the moment began to take on an entirely different shape.

Words like: 'Do you have any conception of what those two weeks are going to mean to me? The problems they are going to cause?'

Had his father laid down an ultimatum during Raschid's last visit home? Was that why those two weeks had been so important?

'And what does rumour say, exactly?' she asked carefully.

Changing gear with a flourish, he sent her a small grimace. 'That he has a month to sort his life out before he goes home to marry some cousin of a cousin or some such person. Is it true?' he asked curiously. 'Is that why he's finished it?'

Evie didn't answer. She didn't do anything but sit there staring directly ahead of her while new horrors settled over old horrors. Some cousin of a cousin being the new horror.

For Evie knew all about Aisha. Raschid had never been anything but honest about his cousin of a cousin who had been nothing more than a shadow in the wings of his life while she grew from child to woman enough to marry a prince.

'Are you okay?' Harry asked. 'You've gone awfully pale…'

No, Evie thought. I'm not okay. 'What a mess!' Raschid had muttered. 'What a damned mess!'

He hadn't been joking. The whole thing was a mess! She had already been living on borrowed time with him when she'd broken her news last night.

And, what was worse, she had probably been the last one to know it!

It didn't matter. Nothing seemed to matter any more. It was over. In every which way she looked at it, the affair was most definitely over. She only wished now that she had kept her stupid mouth shut about the baby. At least then she could have walked away from him with some semblance of dignity intact.

Now?

The whole wretched thing was just destined to get ugly. With their families, with the press, between themselves.

For she was not going to go down in history as the woman who held her Arab sheikh lover to ransom with a baby! Evie grimly promised herself. And Raschid, she was sure, was not going to go down in history as the Arab sheikh who deserted his pregnant mistress to marry elsewhere!

The car ate up the miles while Evie sat there so sunk in

the wallowing mire of her own muddy thinking that she wasn't aware of the frequent worried glances Harry kept on sending her, or what he was seeing when he did look at her.

She didn't look well. There were bruises around her eyes and a white ring of tension around her mouth. Her skin was too pale, and her fingers trembled where they rested on her lap.

They arrived in Chelsea where her mews cottage stood only a short walk away from the World Aid Foundation, where she worked on a purely voluntary basis, drumming up gifts of money from the wealthy.

The cottage belonged to Julian. It was one of several properties the family owned in and around London. Her mother resided in something similar in Kensington. And Julian himself used a classy apartment not far from Hyde Park.

Great to have money, Evie bleakly acknowledged. Great to able to do what you wanted when you wanted to do it without having to consider the cost.

Great to know that she could bring up her baby without having to accept a single penny from Raschid to do it, she tagged on cynically.

The car had stopped. Looking around a little dazedly, Evie realised that Harry had already got out and was striding towards the boot.

She climbed out too, the sunlight just managing to seep over the rooftops feeling warm on her icy face. Walking to the back of the car, she waited until Harry had closed the boot lid then went to take her bag from him.

'Thanks for the lift, Harry. I...'

The bag was swung out of her reach. 'I'm coming in with you,' he insisted.

'But your foal. You should...'

'The least you can do is offer me a cup of coffee for my trouble,' he pointed out gently.

'Of course, I'm sorry,' she murmured contritely, and turned to cross the pavement to her white-painted front door.

The telephone was ringing even as she stepped into the house with Harry right behind her. Evie froze where she stood, counting off the rings until the answering machine took over. Her voice sounded strange to her own ears as the machine chanted out her recorded message. A moment after that and her mother's voice came whipping across the room towards her.

'Evie, I don't know what you think you're playing at, walking out like this. God knows what the Beverleys are going to think!' A sigh rasped like sandpaper across the room. 'I don't care what a mess your private life is in, this is so bad-mannered! Now I suppose I will have to make up excuses for you. It just isn't fair, Evie! Don't you think I spend enough time making excuses for you as it is?'

Another sigh, then came a few tense moments when nothing happened while her mother seemed to be getting a hold on her temper. 'Look,' she said, sounding marginally less aggressive. 'Call me here when you get home. I need to know you arrived there safely...'

'You didn't tell her you came away with me?' Harry asked when the call had finished.

Evie shook her head. 'I just said I'd got a lift home,' she explained, forcing her stiff legs to move towards the kitchen.

She hadn't wanted to involve Harry's name in all of this; it would cause too many complications when things were complicated enough. Her mother didn't need any help to cast Harry in the role of saviour. Give Lucinda an inch and she would take a mile...

'Are you going to call her back?'

Evie didn't answer. Instead she picked up the kettle and took it over to the sink to fill it with fresh water. She didn't

want to talk to anyone—not even Harry—though it would
be churlish under the circumstances to tell him that.

'Evie…'

The phone started ringing again, cutting off whatever
Harry had been about to say and turning Evie to stone
again where she stood clutching the kettle while she waited
to hear who was trying to contact her this time.

A moment after that and Raschid's voice came, sounding hard and tight and very, very weary. 'Pick up the
phone, Evie,' he commanded. 'I know you are there…'

Evie didn't move. The seconds ticked by, the silence
picking at tautly stretched nerve-ends.

'Evie!' Impatience roughened his voice now. 'This is
foolish! You are being foolish! Pick up the phone!'

'How does he know you are here?' Harry asked curiously. 'Would your mother have told him?'

Incapable of speech, Evie gave a small shake of her
head. Her mother would rather die than tell Raschid anything. No, Raschid must have seen her leave, she decided.

Like herself, she presumed, he must have spent a lousy
sleepless night wondering what the hell he was going to
do about her, and had probably been staring out of his
bedroom window when she and Harry took off together.

A disembodied sigh rushed impatiently around the room
when her refusal to comply made Raschid angry. Teeth
clenched, body—the very muscles that made her heart
beat—all locked into a dreadful straining paralysis, Evie
waited to hear what was going to come next.

'I am on my way to you,' he grimly informed her.
'Make sure you get rid of that fool who is there with you,
or I will not be responsible for what may happen to him!'

'What the…?' Harry burst out in disbelief.

Snap, the line went dead. Evie jumped, almost dropping
the kettle.

'How did he know I was here?' Harry gasped. 'Does
the man have special powers or something?'

'Or something,' Evie tightly replied. And from being frozen the muscles around her heart were now accelerating wildly as anger began to take her over. Putting down the kettle, she walked out of the open-plan kitchen and across the sitting room to glance out of the window.

There were several cars parked in the mews, but only one had somebody sitting inside it.

'He must have seen us leave Beverley together,' she told Harry as he came to stand beside her. Then she nodded her head towards the occupied car. 'There is the object of his special powers,' she dryly concluded.

'You mean—he's having you watched?' Harry was beginning to look hunted. 'But why should he bother to do that? The man is marrying another woman!'

But this one is having his baby, Evie added grimly to herself as she winced at Harry's thoughtless reminder.

'Look,' she said, turning towards him, 'I'm very grateful to you for bringing me home. But I think you should leave before he gets here.'

'I'm not leaving you alone with him!' he declared, coming over all macho and protective. 'The man sounded damned dangerous,' he added. 'For all I know, he may have plans to spirit you away to his harem, or something.'

Evie allowed herself a wry smile at that scenario— though the real joke of it was that Raschid might well be planning to do just that. She wasn't sure. She didn't understand him any more. After two years of believing that she knew him inside out and back to front, she was now discovering that he had hidden depths she had never allowed for.

The main one being his determination to hang on to something that he hadn't even wanted.

The baby—the baby. Not Evie or what they felt for each other, but a baby that he deemed as his possession. And it wasn't in Raschid's nature to let go of something he believed belonged to him.

So, maybe the harem theory wasn't so far-fetched.
Maybe he could see her hidden away there with only his
eunuchs for company while his new wife lived in complete
ignorance of her new husband's intimate prisoner.

Or maybe not so ignorant, Evie then amended, remem-
bering his sister Ranya's meek obedience to the men in
her life.

A different world, a different culture, a different view
of life.

She shuddered.

'He's started the car engine,' Harry said.

Evie turned to see tell-tale blink of an amber indicator—
and felt a tiny quiver of alarm go slinking through her
blood. It could only mean that Raschid was mere seconds
away.

'Harry—!' she pleaded urgently. 'Get out of here before
Raschid arrives. Please...'

'But—'

'But nothing,' Evie interrupted, already moving to open
the front door. 'He won't hurt me, but I can't say what he
may do to you.'

She was nervous, she was anxious. Harry didn't like the
look of either. And her slender fingers had that open front
door in a death grip.

A black Mercedes drove slowly by them.

'Take the lady's advice,' a deep voice dropped smoothly
into the tension. 'She knows what she is talking about...'

They both jumped, both turned, both stared at the man
who was now filling the doorway.

# CHAPTER SIX

DRESSED entirely in black—black jeans, black tee shirt, soft black leather jacket—he looked mean and he looked dangerous. Evie stared at him and felt her mouth go dry, felt her skin begin to prickle, and felt that terrible sizzle of sexual attraction rush through her blood as it always did when she looked at him.

'Raschid—' she began warningly.

He ignored her. His attention was fixed upon poor Harry who was beginning to look a little hot around his shirt collar.

'Evie needed a lift,' Harry explained, trying to sound belligerent but only managing to sound defensive.

'And we thank you for your time and effort,' Raschid responded politely. 'But I believe you have a rather valuable mare in need of your personal attention. So we will understand your desire to rush off...'

As a dismissal it just about said it all, but what struck Evie harder was the fact that Raschid knew all about Harry's pregnant mare.

Maybe he did possess the second sight, she thought a little breathlessly, her eyes locked with unwilling fascination on those narrowed golden eyes of his.

'Now, just a minute...' Harry decided to dig his heels in.

Evie flicked her gaze in his direction and almost groaned when she saw the sudden stubborn jut of his chin. Harry might be a shy and self-effacing kind of person, but, like Raschid, he had been born to cherish his own high station.

'You can't just—'

'No, Harry.' It was Evie who stopped him, Evie who

knew that if it came to a hands-on battle Harry would lose out on all counts, and that included his pride. Without thinking what she was doing, she stepped up to him and touched his cheek with gentle fingertips to gain his attention then sent him a sad, apologetic smile. 'You've done enough,' she told him softly.

'But he—'

This time Evie stopped the words by placing her lips against his. It startled him enough to render him silent. Behind her she could feel Raschid's anger reaching out towards her like tentacles that wanted to rip her apart for daring to kiss another man in front of him like this. She ignored the sensation. Ignored the man.

'I am very grateful for what you've done, but it really is best that you leave now. Please, Harry.' She pleaded with him when she saw the stubbornness still setting his jaw.

Indecision began to cloud his grey eyes. 'You will be okay?' he asked, ignoring the way Raschid stiffened at the question.

Evie smiled reassuringly and nodded. 'I'll call you,' she promised as an added incentive. 'Later on today.'

Another few moments of high-tension silence, then Harry reluctantly gave in. His hands came up to cup Evie's shoulders, his head lowering so he could place a brief kiss against her mouth, then he was letting her go and with a cold nod of his head in Raschid's direction he stepped out of the cottage and walked off towards his car.

Evie's sense of relief was very short-lived. She glanced at Raschid who was looking back at her with narrowed eyes that were not pleasant. Alarm went tingling down her backbone.

'Very touching,' he drawled, holding her defiant gaze captive as he stepped into the cottage and closed the door behind him. 'Little scenes like that force me to wonder if I asked all the wrong questions last night.'

'I don't recall you asking any questions,' Evie replied with tight derision.

'No?' As threatening as hell, he took a step towards her, mouth thin, eyes as hard as pebbles. 'Then allow me to ask this one,' he requested. 'Is the baby mine?'

It took several moments for the question to sink in, and even when it did Evie continued to stand there staring at him in stunned disbelief. Then they came—the anger, the sense of personal offence; they swam up from the very depths of her loins to course like fire through her blood.

'How *dare* you?' she breathed in shimmering fury.

'Answer the question,' he demanded thinly.

His eyes were glittering, his bared teeth gleaming white between the taut stretch of his lips. Evie stared into those threatening gold eyes, and saw the word traitor blazing from them.

'It's not yours,' she said, turned her back on him and walked away, leaving him standing there with his arrogant guns most satisfyingly spiked for once.

The cottage wasn't big, just one long room really, split into two by a breakfast bar that separated the kitchen from the living room. The living-room window looked out on the cobbled street at the front of the cottage, the rear window on a tiny walled garden. It was nothing more than an old-fashioned back yard, alive at the moment with summer blooms planted by herself in hanging baskets and an array of terracotta tubs.

It was to that rear window that Evie went, leaning her slender hips against the built-in unit and folding her arms across her front while she stared out at the flower-filled little garden with absolutely no pleasure whatsoever.

The reason why she was feeling no pleasure in what was on show outside was that she was feeling no pleasure in anything right now.

'Liar.' Raschid's smooth voice dripped with a dry lazy confidence.

Evie grimaced, not in the least bit surprised that it had taken him mere seconds to work that one out. Turning round, she found him standing in the opening between the kitchen and living room.

His jacket had gone, his casual stance as he leaned a broad shoulder against the wall beside him a masterpiece in long, fluid, muscular lines. Nothing about him was left wanting. Not the cut of his silky dark hair or the colour of his beautiful skin or even the casual clothes that covered a body built to god-like proportions.

He was Man personified—to Evie at least. And the real point here was that he knew it. Which was why he could call her a liar so confidently.

'Rumour has it,' she continued, 'that marriage to the cousin of a cousin looms large upon your horizon.'

That made his eyes narrow slightly, fixed his attention on her cool expression that was challenging him to dare deny the charge.

Of course, he didn't deny it. 'Marriage to Aisha has always loomed large on my horizon, Evie; you know that,' he answered levelly. 'I have never tried to hide it from you.'

'Until last night,' Evie said bitterly.

'Is that why you ran away with the Marquis this morning?' he demanded. 'Because you heard a rumour that may or may not have been true?'

He wasn't denying it, though. 'I ran away because I didn't want another ugly scene with you.'

He sighed—which was something, she supposed, and at last began to look as weary as she felt. 'But we have to talk this through, and you know that, Evie.'

Oh, yes, she thought heavily. She knew that. But Raschid's idea of talking was to give orders that she was supposed to obey.

'I need time to myself, to decide what I want to do,' she told him huskily.

'Time is something I don't have,' he countered very grimly.

'Because your father has issued you with an ultimatum?' she asked.

His shrug was eloquent, his indifference to the question more so. 'As I am going to marry you, the question of my marrying anyone else is therefore rendered useless.'

Given just who and what he was, Evie wasn't so sure about that.

Turning away again, she went back to filling and plugging in the kettle. Behind her she could feel Raschid watching her, trying to calculate her mood and what she was thinking. It didn't take much perception to see that, despite his reaffirmation about marriage, Evie was still not accepting it as the natural solution.

'They say your father is ill again,' she remarked, reaching into the cupboard for the caddy of his favourite mint tea without really knowing she was doing it.

'He has to undergo some open heart surgery,' Raschid confirmed. 'But he is refusing to do so until I am safely married and settled in his seat of power.'

'Which you won't be if you marry me.'

'I cannot lie and say that people are going to be delighted,' Raschid sombrely acknowledged. 'But given time they will become used to the idea. We all will,' he added carefully.

Meaning her, Evie supposed.

The teapot was special, more a tiny silver urn that Asim had given her as a gift last year when she had got him to show her how to prepare the mint tea the way Raschid liked it.

It had been a nice thought—a caring thought. But even Asim, whom she was perhaps closer to than anyone else attached to Raschid, would stare in horror at his master actually marrying her.

'I won't marry you, Raschid,' she said, spooning the

pale green coarse-cut leaves into the urn. 'It would be wrong for me and disastrous for you.'

'Define disastrous,' he requested.

One of those weary sighs whispered from her. 'Your country's stability depends upon its Muslim roots,' she explained. 'Marrying a Christian would weaken those roots. Which is why the cousin of a cousin has always hovered in the shadows throughout the time we've been together.'

He didn't bother to argue the point, which made her want to weep. 'Now explain why it would be wrong for you?' he prompted instead.

Another sigh—one that was caught back before it was uttered this time, but her heart lay heavy in her breast as she stood there watching the kettle come slowly to the boil. 'You would stifle me. The situation would stifle me. As our relationship stands at the moment I have the freedom to do more or less as I please. The restrictions placed on a Muslim wife are stifling enough, but for one who would be as disapproved of as I would be... I would suffocate,' she predicted.

'And the child you carry?' he continued levelly. 'What is supposed to happen to him while you protect yourself from a stifling marriage and save my country from instability?'

He was mocking her but angrily. He didn't like the picture she was painting but couldn't come up with a better one to paint over it.

'The he may be a she,' she smiled. 'Which would not be so big a problem, would it?'

'We are not barbarians, Evie,' he said tightly. 'We do not drown our female offspring at birth, I promise you.'

'I'm pleased to hear it,' she said, pouring boiling water into the urn. 'Tell me...what would your people think of a half English boy child who would in effect be his father's heir if we married?'

'He will be my heir whether or not we marry,' Raschid

informed her with a grimness that had Evie spinning round
to stare at him in horror.

'No, Raschid!' she cried out in protest. 'You—'

'Watch out!' he rasped at her.

But it was already too late. 'Oh, damn!' Evie gasped as
pain like nothing she had ever felt in her life before forced
the air to rush from her lungs.

She hadn't even realised she still had hold of the hot
urn! The jerky way she had spun around had sent the hot
tea shooting out of the spout and over her arm.

'Here!' Raschid was suddenly in front of her and grab-
bing hold of her hand to yank her over to the sink. Ice-
cold water gushed over burning hot skin, sending heart-
stopping shock waves shooting through her system.

Her eyes were closed, and she was shaking so badly that
even her teeth chattered. If Raschid hadn't been holding
her up with his arm clamped around her waist, she would
have fallen in a trembling heap to the tiled floor.

'Did it splash you anywhere else?' he asked harshly.

It was all she could do to shake her head. She felt sick,
she felt dizzy, the shock and the pain driving her to breathe
in choked whimpers.

Raschid hissed out something nasty from between violently clenched teeth. 'You fool,' he muttered, ruthless in
his determination to keep her arm beneath the agonising
coldness of the water. 'Did I ask for tea—did I? If you've
damaged this beautiful skin I will throttle you!'

'Sh-shut up,' she breathed, in too much pain to want to
listen to him taking his own distress out on her.

'I should have seen it coming!' he railed on regardless.
'When you play the super-controlled ice-maiden, it usually
means you're struggling to keep yourself together for one
reason or another!'

Well, she wasn't together now, Evie thought painfully.
She was literally coming apart at the seams. Her arm hurt,
her body hurt and her heart hurt. 'I w-won't marry you,'

she choked out, his remark reminding her why she had ended up scalding herself like this.

The hand clamped around her slender wrist tightened its grip, then grimly lowered the arm into a sink now full of icy water before he let go of her. The tap was switched off, Evie wilted weakly against the unit, her body sliding away from his until she was hunched over the sink with her arm immersed up to the armpit.

Leaving her standing there weak and shaking, fighting to keep the sickness, the dizziness and now the onset of wretched tears at bay, Raschid strode angrily away. A moment later she heard him running up the stairs, and a minute after that and he was back with the first-aid box from her bathroom and a snowy white towel, both of which he angrily tossed down on the unit beside her.

Then he was gently lifting her arm out of the water and laying it on the towel. He didn't speak as he bent over to inspect the damage, but his face was cast in stone, his eyes glittering from between lushly curling lashes, his mouth nothing but a thin tight line.

She watched his brown fingers move gently over the reddened area of her arm, watched him carefully cover it with the towel then turn to open the first-aid box.

Most of the heat had been neutralised by the water by then, although Evie still could not stop shaking. Producing a tube of antiseptic, he deftly unscrewed the cap then began lightly smearing the ointment on her arm.

'Does that hurt?'

She shook her head in answer.

'If it blisters we will have to call in a burns specialist. But at the moment you seem to have been lucky.'

Lucky, Evie thought. There had to be an irony in that somewhere though she didn't feel like looking for it.

'Raschid—please listen to me,' she pleaded. 'You can't—'

He glanced up, those golden eyes so hard they silenced

her utterly. 'Don't force me to get tough with you,' he warned. 'For you will not like the tactics I will employ.'

'Was that a threat?' she gasped.

He didn't answer, didn't need to while he continued to look at her like that. Raschid had a ruthless streak running through him that could, when invited, become quite cruel—though until now Evie had never been a party to that side of him.

'The child is mine.' He reinforced the main points of conflict here. 'You are mine. I have not the slightest intention of giving either of you up. Which means I must make your place in my life official.'

'And damn the consequences?'

He grimaced but nodded. 'And damn the consequences,' he flatly confirmed.

The phone began to ring, slicing through the tension like a knife.

'Do you want me to answer it?' Raschid asked quietly.

Evie shook her head, her eyes lowered while she waited for the answer machine to take over.

It was her mother again. 'Have you seen this morning's paper?' Her shrill voice slashed across the room. 'I have never been so embarrassed in all my life! If it isn't bad enough that you disappear without a word of thanks to anyone, that wretched man only goes and does the same thing—then I have to contend with the pair of you staring out at me from the front page of the newspaper!'

Evie looked up at Raschid, a question in her eyes, but he shook his dark head in grim answer.

'I'm telling you, Evie,' her mother said tightly. 'I am so darned angry with you I could very easily disown you! Front page you stand wrapped in his arms! Centre page he stands with his father announcing his upcoming marriage to another woman!'

Raschid hissed out an acrid curse, his big frame taut as he strode across the room towards the telephone. He was about to snatch it up to demand what the hell Lucinda was talking about when her voice came again.

'And where is the picture of Julian and Christina?' she demanded tearfully. 'Nowhere to be seen! Scandal—that's all you've ever brought me, Evangeline! Pain, disillusionment, embarrassment and scandal! The Beverleys are upset and trying not to show it! I am upset and trying not to show it! But where are you? That's what I would like to know! With him somewhere? Are the pair of you nicely holed up enjoying your last passionate tryst before he dumps you to marry someone else? Perhaps you would like the press to cover that shocking event too!'

The connection was severed. In the drumming silence that followed it, Evie stood cradling her towel-wrapped arm against her and wondered bleakly what her mother was going to say when she found out about the coming baby.

A loud knock suddenly sounded on the front door. Evie jumped violently, the air shivering out of her lungs as she automatically walked forward to go and answer it.

'No,' Raschid bit out forcefully. 'Check who it is first.'

Diverting towards the window, Evie glanced out then gave a gasp of surprise. 'It's the press!' she exclaimed, and began quickly dragging the curtains across the glass when half a dozen of them saw her and began converging on the living-room window.

Within seconds the noise was unbelievable, people knocking on the door and on the window, calling out her name and shouting out questions. White-faced, she turned towards Raschid. 'What's going on?' she asked bewilderedly. 'What was my mother talking about? Why are they here?'

'I don't know.' Frowning, he was already lifting the telephone up and stabbing in a set of numbers.

Evie stood, still trembling with shock from her scalding without the added confusion that was now taking place outside her home. Raschid's voice was tight with anger as he spoke in his own language to whoever it was he had contacted, his dark face growing darker by the second, while the thumping on the door and window grew so loud Evie could barely hear herself even think.

On a violent curse, Raschid slammed down the receiver. At the same moment a newspaper was pushed through the letterbox. It landed on the doormat with an ominous thud. Evie went to get it but Raschid was there before her.

'Do you have anything to say about this, Miss Delahaye?' a muffled voice shouted through the letterbox. 'Front page. Can't miss it!' the voice added helpfully.

Front page. Can't miss it.

Evie stood by Raschid's arm and simply stared at what she was seeing. It was a photograph of herself and Raschid kissing beneath the wedding canopy at Beverley. Above it the headline read: 'Is This Farewell?' Below it was the sub-heading: 'Behran Embassy announces the forthcoming marriage of Sheikh Raschid Al Kadah to neighbouring sheikh's daughter! The marriage will unite two of the most powerful sheikhdoms and effectively put Evie Delahaye out in the cold.'

'This has not been announced with my approval!' Raschid insisted forcefully. 'My father is attempting to force my hand!'

'Oh, no,' Evie whispered, sinking into the nearest chair when her legs went weak beneath her.

Raschid stood gripping the newspaper between white-knuckled fists while he read on, his dark face locked up like a steel trap. Neither spoke again; neither needed to. They both knew very well what this was going to mean to them.

For, no matter how much he would like to deny what his father had announced, Evie knew Raschid dared not. To deny it would be tantamount to insulting both his own father and Aisha's family.

So this is it, Evie concluded hollowly. Her instincts had been sending her all the right signals, and this was the end for her and Raschid.

No more mouthing words that she didn't really mean. No more pretending she wouldn't marry him. For it was only now as she sat here accepting that she could never marry him that she realised she had been pretending to herself.

And it hit her hard, so hard she could barely function.

The telephone began ringing again. Neither of them heard it. Just as they didn't hear the pounding on the front door and the window any more. For those few stark minutes the very walls could have come tumbling down around them and neither would have moved a muscle.

Then the letterbox flew up and a pair of eyes appeared in the opening. 'Did you know about this yesterday, Miss Delahaye?' a voice demanded. 'Is that why you and the Sheikh were careful to avoid each other at your brother's wedding?'

Not careful enough, was Evie's hollow answer to that as she thought of that revealing photograph. And we didn't avoid each other, she reminded herself as, with glassy eyes, she watched Raschid throw down the newspaper and angrily reach for one of her cream linen easy chairs. Picking it up, he rammed it against the door, effectively trapping the letterbox shut.

We danced together, her own train of thought went on uninterrupted. We made love in my room before we went to the ball together.

Raschid had been angry with her for avoiding him. He hadn't known about this then, she was sure of it. For, whatever he was, he was not devious.

Angry again later, yes, when she told him about the baby, she acknowledged. Seeing all the problems a baby was going to cause because his father was already laying the pressure on him to marry Aisha.

But this—this was cruel. This did not take into account her own feelings. This publicly stripped her of her pride and left her heart exposed and bleeding.

Raschid just wouldn't have done that to her.

'I'll go away,' she whispered as one thought led haphazardly on to another. 'I have relatives in Australia. I can—'

'No!' Raschid ground out at her furiously.

Glancing up, she saw him through a haze of tears. His wonderful skin had lost most of its colour, his eyes standing out like two golden suns locked into fierce eruption. 'You will do nothing—nothing until I can get this sorted out! There is a way—there has to be a way!' he raked out hoarsely.

And it was that hoarseness of voice that cut her to the quick. For Raschid, like herself, knew the emptiness of that statement.

Outside, the noise was growing. Inside someone was shouting questions at her via the answering machine. With an angry jerk, Raschid bent down and pulled the plug on the phone.

Then, on a growl, he muttered, 'We've got to get out of here,' and retrieved his leather jacket to take his mobile phone out of one of the pockets. Tossing the jacket aside again, he stepped into the kitchen to peer out of the rear window, looking to see if they had been besieged at the rear of the cottage as well as the front.

No tell-tale camera lens came poking over the top of the seven-foot-high brick wall that protected the back of the property.

'Get the car around the back of the cottage,' he rasped tersely to whoever he was speaking to. 'Keep the engine running and be prepared to move.'

With that he came back to Evie's side, bent to grasp her uninjured arm and lifted her to her feet. 'Come on,' he urged grimly.

'But—'

She looked dazed and shaken. Raschid shook his dark head. 'You can't stay here,' he clipped out. 'And I certainly cannot. Going by the questions they have been throwing at you, I don't think they even know I am here—which is to our advantage. I arrived before they did, and my car was parked around the corner. With a bit of luck,' he added as he unbolted the back door and pulled it open, 'we can be out of here before they realise you've escaped.'

'Escaped to where?' Evie asked bleakly as he pushed her outside and followed her, pulling the door shut behind him.

'To my apartment,' he replied as if the question had been a serious one and not a stark response to her own bleak sense of isolation. 'At least there I can protect you from all of this until we decide what we are going to do.'

Do? Evie let out a nervy little laugh that verged on the hysterical. They both knew what he had to do. It was her future that was hanging in the balance here.

# CHAPTER SEVEN

IT WAS another warm sunny day and the enclosed back yard acted like a suntrap. But Evie felt shivering cold as she let Raschid take her over to the solid wooden back gate that led out into the narrow alleyway, which ran right along the row of terraced cottages.

They paused there in the sunshine, Raschid sliding back the two bolts that secured the gate then going still with his hand on the latch while he listened for the sound of his car arriving. Evie stood beside him with her face lowered where she stared blankly at the white towel still covering her scalded arm. The skin was burning a little, but it didn't seem to matter, not when her whole world felt as though it was slowly but surely falling in on her.

Raschid put a hand to her waist, then sent it travelling up her trembling spine until it reached her nape where his long fingers gently closed so he could use his thumb beneath her chin to lift her eyes to his.

Her heart turned over at the dark glow she could see burning in his eyes. He was so handsome, she thought tragically, so dark and smooth and so right for her somehow—how was she ever going to survive without him?

'I love you,' he murmured huskily. 'Don't let anyone or anything ever try to convince you otherwise.'

And he did love her. Evie only had to look into those rich golden eyes to know it was true love that burned from them.

'But love isn't enough, is it?' she said, her mouth quivering on the true wretchedness of that comment.

Bending his head, he caught her quivering mouth, tasted it—soothed it with his own firmer lips. 'I will find a way through this,' he gruffly vowed. 'You are mine. I am yours. Nothing can change that.'

Evie wished with all her aching heart that she could believe that—but she couldn't. 'Duty can,' she replied.

Raschid didn't answer but his expression clouded—and she couldn't even swallow against the thickness that was suddenly clogging her throat.

The car drew up beyond the gate then. Lifting the latch, Raschid stepped out to check the alleyway before he opened the rear door of a silver Mercedes then quickly urged Evie inside.

'Right—go!' he commanded the driver as he got in beside her.

It was the sheer urgency in his voice that made Evie turn to look through the car's rear window. A man with half a dozen cameras hanging around his neck had just appeared at the other end of the alleyway. He was desperately trying to bring one of those cameras up to his face as they took off across the cobbles at speed.

'It's all right,' Raschid soothed, seeing Evie's anxious expression. 'He is on foot. By the time he has collected his own form of transport we will be gone.'

'But he now knows you're with me,' she pointed out heavily. Which made for just another bit of delicious scandal for them to feed upon.

'I will always be with you,' he replied with a flat-voiced sincerity that only helped to heighten her anxiety.

For how could he make a pronouncement like that knowing it was only going to cause more distress for all of them?

'Raschid—'

'No.' His hand came out, reaching across the small gap separating them to close warmly around one of her own tightly clenched hands. 'We will not discuss this now,' he ordained. 'You are too upset and I am too confused by what my father has done for either of us to discuss anything constructively.'

'But—'

'But,' he intruded, turning dark eyes on her that issued one very dire warning, 'you are carrying my child, Evie, which is one fact we are not in any confusion about. And that child will have my name no matter how many problems we have to surmount to reach that goal.'

A vow from the soul that filled her breast with warm honeyed love for this man who valued her so dearly.

But it didn't stop her mind from gnawing away at the problems they were about to face as the car reached the end of the alleyway and shot out on to the main street, heading towards the river.

The sound of Raschid's mobile phone bursting into life brought her sharply to attention. His hand left hers, and for the next few minutes he talked at length in his own language. His voice sounded hard, the answers he was receiving to any questions he shot out doing nothing to ease his temper.

'They're all over the place,' he muttered when he eventually sat back again. 'Besieging my apartment block as well as your cottage! I could really have done without all of this!'

*He* could? Evie's head was beginning to swim with it all. 'You got me out of my house so fast, I haven't even got my purse,' she said, adding to his problems. 'And we didn't lock the doors behind us.'

'Your cottage will have been secured within minutes of us leaving,' Raschid assured her. 'And you can survive without your purse, surely?'

He was terse to the point of being cutting, and Evie turned her face sideways and pretended he wasn't there. She wasn't hurt or offended by his tone; in fact she sympathised with it. The whole situation had exploded into something way beyond what either of them could control, and that was what was so hard to swallow.

Being out of control.

'How is your arm?'

Evie glanced down at it, rather confused to see it was still wrapped in the white towel. 'It still burns a little,' she replied.

But then, so did her eyes; they felt sore and gritty through lack of sleep and a dire need to sob her heart out. Perhaps he knew it, because, on a heavy sigh, Raschid slid across the gap separating them so he could pull her against him.

'Asim will take care of your arm as soon as we reach my apartment,' he murmured. 'All we need to do first is get past the press waiting for us there, and that should be easy enough when they cannot follow us underground, into the car park.'

'Then what?' she asked. 'Do we hide away like fugitives in your apartment instead of my cottage?' There didn't seem to be much difference between the two locations to Evie.

'At least I can protect you there,' he countered. 'Because,' he then added very grimly, 'this is only the beginning of it all, not the end of it.'

The beginning, not the end. Evie shuddered. 'Sometimes I wish I'd never met you,' she sighed.

Surprisingly he laughed, albeit ruefully. 'Only sometimes?' he mocked. 'There is a chance for us yet, then.'

It was merely one of those light, throw-away remarks people made in times of trouble that really did not mean anything in particular. But still, it weighed heavily on Evie's mind as the car swept up to the security-protected entrance to his basement car park, because she didn't think they had a chance whichever way you looked at it.

Evie sank deeply into the rear seat when she saw the gaggle of press people standing around waiting for them, and Raschid's arm drew her tighter against him as he clipped out a terse order to his driver to run them over if he had to.

Luckily such a dire response wasn't necessary; as the car drove towards them the rat-pack parted, their cameras flashing against the car windows as it forged its way down into the relative sanctuary of the basement.

The car stopped and Raschid jumped out to stride around the car so he could open Evie's door for her. The lift waited; they entered it together and travelled upwards in complete silence. It stopped and the doors slid open directly into Raschid's private white marbled foyer.

Asim was standing there waiting for them. When he saw the way Evie was cradling her towel-wrapped arm he gasped in horror. 'Someone has harmed you, Miss Delahaye?' he asked sharply.

'I did it myself,' Evie dryly replied.

'Hot tea,' Raschid inserted tightly. 'From that urn you gave to her.'

It was a rotten thing to say, especially when poor Asim suddenly looked as if he'd poured the stupid tea over her himself. 'Stop taking your bad temper out on Asim!' she snapped. 'It's not his fault your life is in such a mess!'

'What a damned mess!' he had rasped at her last night. And just now he had added an apt little rider to that with his, 'This is only the beginning of it all, not the end of it.'

Without waiting for instruction, Asim quietly bade Evie to follow him into the living room where he sat her down on one of the chairs then squatted in front of her so he could gently unwrap her burned arm.

The skin looked red, but it hadn't blistered, although when he touched a cool fingertip to it she jumped in pained response. 'It is still hot?' he asked.

Evie nodded her head, weak tears suddenly flooding her eyes.

'Do something about it!' Raschid grated from behind the older man.

'Of course.' As impassive as ever in the face of Raschid's anger, Asim rose up and moved quietly away.

'You're horrible to him,' Evie snapped out accusingly. 'Ever speak to me like that and I will slap your face!'

'Before you burst into tears or after?' he countered. Then sighed and turned his back on her, his stance taut and angry. 'I don't like to see you hurting,' he tagged on gruffly.

Well, I'm hurting in a whole lot of other places you don't even know about, Evie thought bleakly.

Asim came back. Raschid looked relieved. Squatting down in front of her again, the older man unscrewed the top off a jar and began gently smearing a clear ointment on her scalded skin.

It was delicious, so cooling. Evie sighed softly and relaxed back in the chair to close her aching eyes. A few minutes later a moist bandage was being carefully wrapped around her arm.

'The heat is receding?' Asim asked her.

She nodded. 'Thank you, Asim.'

'We will repeat the process again later,' he said. 'But for now, Miss Delahaye, I really think you should lie down on the bed and rest. You are looking exceedingly pale...'

'But—'

'Good advice.' Raschid was suddenly standing over her.

'But...' she tried again.

'But nothing. To put it bluntly, Evie, you look dreadful.'

She felt it too—shock, she assumed, the delayed kind of shock that was making her feel ever so slightly woozy. 'I haven't had a single thing to eat today,' she remembered as Raschid helped her get to her feet.

'Then while we get you comfortable in bed Asim will prepare something—what would you like?'

It was weird, but having felt her stomach growling for

want of sustenance, it was suddenly churning for an entirely different reason. 'Oh, no,' she choked, bringing her hand up to cover her mouth.

'What's the matter?' Raschid demanded sharply.

But Evie had already broken free from him to run.

A single glass of water drunk at five-thirty that morning was no real problem to bring back up, but Evie remained leaning over the bowl in the bathroom for a long while afterwards, still feeling sick and dizzy enough not to dare to move away.

After a while, she straightened carefully and went in search of the minty mouthwash she knew Raschid kept hidden behind the large mirrored wall cupboard. Finding it, she shut the cupboard door and was just about to unscrew the cap when a reflection in the mirror caught her attention.

And it came as a shock to see that both Raschid and Asim were standing in the bathroom doorway gravely watching her.

'Oh, go away!' she cried out on a sudden loss of dignity. 'Can't a girl even be sick in private here?'

'We were concerned,' Raschid said.

'Well, don't be,' she snapped, then sighed as her stomach made another grasping clutch at her. 'It happens,' she added fatalistically.

A baby...she thought dazedly. They had made a baby. Lifting her eyes, she stared at Raschid's sober face through the mirror then turned her gaze to Asim.

He knew, she realised painfully. It had quickly hit him just what was not being said here. And the horror he was having difficulty in disguising brought the weak spill of tears washing into her eyes.

'Oh, damn it,' she choked, and turned away from both the mirror and the two men to tip a small quantity of mouthwash into the plastic cap. But her hand was shaking badly, and she spilled more than she caught in the cap before she had enough to warily swill her mouth with.

'Come on…' Raschid's arm came around her shoulders, his voice deep and heavy as he gently turned her. 'You may feel better if you lie down for a while.'

Quietly dismissing Asim, Raschid led her through to the bedroom, and Evie found she just didn't have enough energy to argue with him when he began to undress her. So she simply let him get on with it, lifting a foot when required or an arm, then finally allowed him to slide her between the cool linen sheets.

'He's going to hate me now,' she murmured dully as Raschid straightened away from her. 'For messing up your life.'

'Don't be foolish,' he admonished, not even pretending to wonder whom it was she was talking about. 'Asim has great affection for you, and you know it.'

As he moved away from her, Evie let her eyes follow him. He went to touch the button on the wall that would bring the curtains swishing across the windows. The instant transformation from bright sunlight to a mellow half-light helped soothe the ache going on behind her weary eyes.

'If he seemed upset,' Raschid continued as he walked back to her, 'then it is because he sees the problems facing us just as clearly as you and I do.'

'Your father will hate me.' Evie was in no mood to be consoled right now. 'My mother will hate me…'

'Shut up,' Raschid said. 'Or I may just decide to exert other methods to rid you of your melancholy.'

Lavender eyes that he expected to slice him in two at such an audacious threat were instead blunted by a vulnerability even Raschid had never seen in them before.

It moved him to see it, touched a painful chord deep inside him that wrenched free the impassive mask he had been wearing, and replaced it with a complexity of emotions, all of which revolved around several different kinds of frustration.

'Oh, what the hell?' he muttered to himself, and with a slick economy of movement his tee shirt came off over his head to reveal that wonderful polished bronze breastplate set between wide, muscled shoulders.

Evie watched him wordlessly as he stripped himself naked, let her eyes feast on every beautiful inch of him as he lifted the sheet and slid into the bed. Her arm lifted in welcome; he coiled himself around her. Their mouths touched briefly, then not so briefly.

'This really isn't the time for this.' Evie made a half-hearted attempt to stem what was already rushing through both of them.

'I blame you,' he informed her arrogantly. 'Seeing you lying here looking so vulnerable and knowing you nurture my child inside you has made me feel most disgustingly macho.'

'I can tell,' she drawled in mocking acknowledgement as her hand slid down the flat plane of her stomach to cover the warm, tight evidence of his feelings.

A shiver ripped through him, the kind of shiver that was always his response to her initial touch of him. 'Then you tell me,' he murmured in sudden seriousness, 'how we give this up when we can't even control it while the world falls in on us.'

'I don't know,' Evie sighed heavily.

'Well, I do,' he said as he pushed her on to her back then carefully placed her bandaged arm out of harm's way before he came to lean over her. 'We stay together. Somehow, some way, I will make it happen,' he vowed. 'You are mine. This child you carry is mine. I will lay claim to you both with pride and with honour. And that, my darling, is my promise to you.'

Fine words, wonderful words. But could he bring them

to fruition? And if he could, at what cost to all of those other things in his life he held so dear to him?

Evie let herself be drawn down into that deep well of sensuality where Raschid's loving always took her, but her mind didn't follow; that remained locked in the tight coil of their problems even as they flew.

# CHAPTER EIGHT

EVIE came swimming up from the deep dark slumber she had escaped into after Raschid had moved away from her, and frowned as her ears picked up on the muffled sound of voices raised in anger.

One was Raschid, sounding cold and cutting. The other was...

'Oh, no.' Her mother.

Groaning, she pulled herself up and out of the bed.

In a flurry of urgency she grabbed the first thing that came to hand—a raspberry-coloured long silk wrap that Raschid must have left out for her, which she dragged on and began tying around her as she hurried, barefoot, towards the bedroom door.

The moment she was out in the hallway she could hear clearly what was being said.

'Love?' her mother was deriding icily. 'Love doesn't take and take without giving back! What have you given back during this affair, Sheikh Raschid?' she demanded. 'For I don't see your reputation lying in shreds at your feet, or you becoming the object of everyone's pity!'

Pity? White-faced and shaken to the roots by the very sound of the word, Evie pulled to a halt beneath the open archway that connected the sumptuous living room with the hallway which led to all the other rooms in Raschid's vast apartment.

Her mother was standing there wearing a snow-white suit that was so dramatically effective against her milk-white skin and pale blonde hair—while Raschid was draped from neck to ankles in the flowing dark blue robes of his native culture.

And the two of them were facing up to each other like two very dangerous substances that should never, ever be allowed to mix. Mutual hostility and dislike was rife.

'Yesterday was supposed to be a very special day for my family,' Lucinda Delahaye continued angrily. 'And, to give Evie her due, she tried her level best to make it that! But you had to come. You had to upstage the bride and groom by getting yourself in the papers as usual. You calmly danced with my daughter while the rumours flew thick and fast about your coming marriage to another woman. And if that wasn't enough your own father had made sure the whole world knew what a gullible little fool Evie is where you are concerned!'

'Try trusting her judgement for a change,' Raschid coolly suggested. 'You never know, you may find that Evie can pleasantly surprise you.'

'Not while she continues this shameful affair with you, she won't.'

'Our shameful affair is none of your business.'

'Why don't you just go home to your oil-rich desert— marry your cousin of a cousin and leave my daughter alone?' her mother cried.

To Evie's horror, Raschid laughed. 'If only you knew,' Raschid murmured dryly.

'Frankly, I don't want to know,' her mother said dismissively. 'All I want to do is speak to my daughter.'

'Evie is resting.' Raschid refused. 'She was feeling— unwell,' he explained. 'She—'

'I'm here,' Evie said, quickly cutting off whatever Raschid might have been going to say by stepping into the room.

They turned together—and slid their gazes over her together, the cold blue eyes in stinging condemnation, while the gold ones were carefully hooded so she couldn't read what they were seeing as they checked her out.

Still, it was like being scrutinised by two tough critics.

So much so that one hand went up to clutch at the gaping lapels of her robe while the other hand ran self-conscious fingers through her tumbled hair.

'What's supposed to be wrong with you?' her mother demanded with deep suspicion.

'N-nothing,' Evie replied, carefully avoiding Raschid's gaze as she stepped further into the room. 'I w-was tired, that's all. Wh-what do you want, Mother?' she asked.

'What do I want?' Lucinda repeated. 'I want to know what you think you are doing, lying in this man's bed while he plans his wedding to another woman! Have you no pride—no shame? Have you even bothered to consider what it has done to your reputation to have openly come here with him today knowing full well what he intends to do?'

'Your tone, Lady Delahaye, leaves a lot to be desired,' Raschid inserted grimly.

'My tone, young man,' Evie's mother countered haughtily, 'is none of your business. I was talking to my daughter, not to you.'

If the antagonism between the two of them got any worse, Evie had a horrible feeling they would start telling each other what they really thought, and she didn't think she could cope with that right now.

'Raschid...' It was to him that she turned to plead anxiously. 'Would you mind giving us a few minutes alone— please?'

He didn't look happy. In fact, he didn't look anything but hard and cold and utterly offended by the request. But Evie couldn't let herself be moved by that look. She might not have the perfect relationship with her mother, but she had no wish to see her demolished by him, which Lucinda certainly would be if Raschid decided to take her on.

'If you wish.' He agreed to her request with an icy politeness that made Evie shiver. And with a stiff bow of his head in her mother's direction he strode from the room, leaving the kind of tension behind him that threatened to suffocate.

'That man is so arrogant, he makes my blood boil,' Lucinda said tightly.

'Your own arrogance wouldn't pass scrutiny,' Evie returned heavily. 'This is Raschid's home,' she pointed out. 'Yet you treated him as if he were the intruder here.'

Stiffening slightly, her mother had the grace to take the criticism without defending herself. 'I don't like him,' was all she said.

And the feeling, Evie thought, is entirely mutual.

'He treats you terribly and you let him get away with it.'

'He treats me beautifully,' Evie declared. 'It's just that you choose not to see it.'

Sighing because this encounter had no hope of being anything but hostile as things presently stood, Evie moved off towards the well-equipped drinks bar and bent to open the chiller door to extract a bottle of still water for herself.

'Can I get you anything, Mother?' she asked as she straightened.

'No, thank you,' her mother replied. Then, on a heavy sigh of her own, Lucinda unbent a little and tossed her white clutch purse to one side before deciding to take an interest in her surroundings.

There was nothing in the room that could be called brash, excessive or lacking taste. The floors were polished maple scattered with beautiful Persian rugs, the furniture a clever mix of off-white fabric and polished stone that was gentle on the eye. And the plain-papered oatmeal walls were hung with a rich display of original oils, mostly depicting sights and scenes from Raschid's own country.

Walking over to one of these paintings, her mother studied it carefully while Evie poured the water into a glass.

'Is this his palace?' Lucinda enquired curiously.

'Yes,' Evie confirmed. 'Or one of them,' she then added.

The Al Kadah family owned several impressive-looking homes similar to the one her mother was studying. But that particular one belonged exclusively to Raschid.

'It possesses a rather dramatic beauty, doesn't it?' her mother opined—a trifle reluctantly. 'All those different shades of gold set against the blue of the ocean and the sky while the place itself seems to rise quite naturally out of the desert as if it has been put there by a force more powerful than man...'

Evie was staring down at the glass. Her mouth felt parched, but her stomach was still queasy enough to make the act of actually swallowing the water a thing she had to convince herself she needed to do.

But she looked up in surprise at her mother's words. 'Raschid designed it himself,' she said, smiling slightly at her mother's sudden start. It didn't particularly please her to discover she had been unwittingly complimenting the enemy. 'He had it built to his own design several years before I met him,' she explained. 'It nestles in the foothills of their mountains where the desert crowds in on two sides and the Persian Gulf on the other...'

'Oh,' was all her mother could think of replying to that. 'The man must have hidden talents.'

More hidden talents than you know, Evie thought wryly, and lifted the glass to her lips. The water went down without causing too much commotion, she noted with relief.

'Come home with me, Evie.'

Glancing up, she saw that her mother had turned to face her and was looking at her with something close to sympathy in her cool lavender eyes.

'To be utterly blunt, darling, you look awful,' Lucinda grimly continued. 'Everyone is worried about you. Julian called me from the airport, he was so concerned when he read about this latest development in this morning's paper, and even Lord Beverley is thoroughly shocked and appalled at the way Sheikh Raschid is using you.'

'Raschid isn't using me,' Evie denied. 'He loves me.'

'Love!' her mother derided in the same way she had derided the word to Raschid's face a few minutes ago. 'The man doesn't know the meaning of the word or he wouldn't be planning to betray you like this!'

'In this case, it isn't me who's been betrayed,' Evie said. 'His father placed that announcement without Raschid's approval.'

'Is that what he told you?' Her mother's scepticism was clear.

But Evie lifted her chin to look right into her mother's disbelieving eyes when she said, 'It's the truth. Raschid wouldn't lie—especially to me.'

'Oh, good grief!' Lucinda Delahaye exclaimed. 'I can't believe you can be so gullible!'

'It has nothing to do with gullibility,' Evie countered. 'But it has everything to do with trust. I trust Raschid to be truthful with me.'

'All right, let us suppose that he does speak the truth,' her mother clipped, deciding to change tack when she saw that stubborn tilt to her daughter's chin that she knew so well. 'What does he intend to do about it?'

Ah, Evie thought, the big question, and she lowered her eyes because she had no clear answer to it.

'Lord Beverley informs me there is no way Raschid can pull out of this marriage now it has been made public,' her mother pushed on. 'Which means that you are out in the cold no matter what Raschid would prefer. His future bride's family will insist upon it as any family would having followed your relationship over the last two years.'

'Do you honestly think I would want to continue our relationship if he did marry someone else?' Evie questioned coolly.

Lucinda didn't answer, but the look on her face certainly said it all for her, and it came as a horrible shock to realise that even her own mother believed she was prepared to sink that low for her love of Raschid.

'Well, I wouldn't,' she snapped, turning away to rid herself of the glass because all of a sudden her stomach was acting up again. But this time it had nothing to do with overwrought hormones.

'Then prove it,' her mother said. 'Put a stop to this now before you lose what is left of your pride! We can go down to Westhaven together,' she suggested, pouncing on the flicker of pain she had caught in Evie's eyes before she turned her back to her. 'Hide away there until all of this blows over!'

'I can't,' Evie whispered, lifting a hand to cover her aching eyes. 'I can't leave him until I know for sure that there is no future for us.'

'Oh, for goodness' sake, Evie!' her mother cried out in angry frustration. Stepping forward, she grabbed hold of Evie's arm so she could spin her round to face her. 'When are you going to—?'

'Aagh!' Evie's strangled shriek of agony slicing through the air utterly silenced her mother.

Where he came from, Evie had no conception, but suddenly Asim was standing right there beside them, and was taking hold of her mother's wrist in a grip that grimly prised her fingers from Evie's arm.

'What on earth...?' Lucinda choked in shocked incredulity.

'Your daughter has an injury to the arm you hold,' Asim answered as he let go of her mother.

'An injury?' Lucinda gasped. 'What kind of injury? What have you people been doing to her?'

'It was an accident.' Raschid's tight voice entered the tension. 'Evie scalded herself this morning.'

'You scalded yourself?' her mother repeated, aiming the stunned question at Evie.

But Evie couldn't answer. She was too busy cradling

her arm where the burning pain was making her feel weak and dizzy. Her face had gone white and her body was trembling with aftershocks of an unbelievable agony.

'Sit down, for goodness' sake!' Raschid raked angrily at her. And before she knew it Evie was being unceremoniously dumped into the nearest chair. 'Asim!' He turned that anger on the servant next. 'Do something!'

With his usual calm, Asim was already squatting down beside Evie and gently taking hold of her arm while Evie just sat, eyes closed, face drained, and shook violently.

'What does he know about burns?' Lucinda put in shrilly.

'More than most,' Raschid gratingly replied.

'But she needs to see a damned doctor!' Lucinda declared in protest as she stood by watching in pulsing horror while Asim began to gently unwrap Evie's injured arm.

In a paper-dry tone that scraped over everyone, Raschid drawled, 'She is seeing one right now.'

It was shocking enough news to bring Evie's eyes open to stare at the servant in dumb disbelief. Asim caught the look and smiled briefly. 'I have been Sheikh Raschid's personal physician since the day he was born,' he quietly explained.

'Well, you old fraud,' she breathed. 'You've let me believe you were nothing more than chief cook and bottle-washer here for the last two years!'

'As you know,' he replied dryly, 'he is rarely ill.'

'Ouch!' she gasped when he touched a particularly tender spot on her arm.

Looking down, she saw that the skin had blistered. Over her head, she heard Raschid mutter something. Her mother, it seemed, had been struck totally speechless.

'A burns specialist, Asim?' Raschid demanded harshly.

'No, sir,' the other man replied. 'But I will need my bag,' he said, getting up. 'If you will excuse me for a moment.'

Walking away, he left an atmosphere behind him that would have split atoms. Raschid stood to one side of Evie, her mother on the other. And Evie herself kept her face lowered because she just didn't feel up to dealing with either of them right now.

'I'm sorry, Evie.' Her mother's voice sounded unsteady. 'I didn't mean to hurt you.'

'I know,' she replied. 'To be honest, I had forgotten about it myself until you touched it.'

'But it looks so dreadful!'

Evie just smiled bleakly to herself because there was no way she could tell her mother that the blisters which were now broken and weeping were where her fingers had gripped.

'Was this what you meant when you said she wasn't well?'

The question was aimed at Raschid, but Evie answered. 'Yes,' she said firmly.

'No,' Raschid coolly contradicted her. 'Evie was feeling unwell because she is pregnant...'

On a sigh that came from the weary depths of her body, Evie sank more deeply into the soft-cushioned chair and closed her eyes again as the new silence that followed that announcement began to explode all around her. And for the space of the next thirty teeth-gritting seconds no one moved, no one spoke, while they waited for her mother's inevitable reaction.

Yet, when it did come, it wasn't what Evie was expecting. She was expecting anger, disgust, even biting condemnation aimed at both of them. What she got was a groan that had her mother sinking heavily into the nearest chair.

'Oh, Evie...' Lucinda sighed out painfully. 'How could you—how could you?'

Evie's eyes snapped open, the tone threading through her words bringing a flash of bright anger into her eyes.

'Are you daring to imply that I got pregnant deliberately?' she demanded.

Her mother didn't need to answer the charge because it was already written in large letters across her pained face.

'I don't believe,' she breathed, hurt—so hurt she couldn't contain it, 'that my own mother could suspect me of doing something so crass!'

'Accidents like this just don't happen in this day and age, Evie.'

'No?' she choked, lurching to her feet like a wounded soldier, with her injured arm cradled against her throbbing breasts. 'Well, just look at me, Mother!' she commanded furiously. 'Because what you are seeing is one hell of an accident!'

'Evie—' It was Raschid who used that rough-toned appeal on her. 'Your mother meant no offence. It was a natural assumption to make...'

Was it? Was it really? she thought, turning flashing eyes on him. 'It hadn't occurred to me before,' she breathed shakily. 'But—have you been secretly thinking the same thing?'

'No,' he sighed, but he looked away from her as he said it, and the horrible realisation that the two people she loved most in the world could think she would sink that low struck a severe enough blow to make her sway where she stood.

And suddenly she knew she had taken enough. Her chin came up, her eyes glassing over as she flicked her gaze from one uncomfortable face to the other. 'I don't think I will ever forgive either of you for this,' she told them.

Then, grimly clinging to what was left of her pride after their mutual slaying of it, she turned and walked away.

Asim was just coming back into the room as Evie swept coldly by him. Whatever passed between him and Raschid via the silent clash of their eyes Evie didn't know or even care. But she had only just sunk weakly down on to the side of the bed when Asim knocked on the bedroom door then let himself into the room.

'I must see to your arm,' he quietly explained.

Evie didn't argue. She didn't say a single thing, in fact, as she allowed Asim to do what he had to do with the broken weals now adorning her arm. But inside her head she was saying a lot—not to Asim but to just about everyone else she could bring to mind.

Her family. Raschid's family. The greedy media who would be oh, so very interested to know what a devious and desperate person she had turned out to be!

'The situation is very stressful for everyone right now,' Asim remarked with his usual diplomatic neutrality as he bent over her arm. 'People say things they come to regret later when things are calmer.'

'Which doesn't mean they weren't speaking the truth when they said them,' Evie pointed out. 'You think I deliberately set out to trap him with this baby,' she then accused him. 'I saw it in your eyes when you were too shocked to hide it.'

Only, she had read his expression for one of simple horror then, not suspicion. Now she knew she was going to see the same expression of horrified pity adorning the shocked features of every single person she looked at from now on.

It made her insides squirm, so much so that she jerked her arm as Asim was reapplying the bandage.

'I hurt you?' he asked sharply.

'Everyone is hurting me,' Evie replied with a wealth of pained anger.

Surprisingly he seemed to understand the remark because he said nothing else and a few moments later he was getting to his feet.

'Can I shower with this?' Evie enquired.

'It would be better if you didn't get the arm wet,' he advised.

She nodded stiffly. 'Then do you think you could arrange a taxi for me while I go and get dressed?'

It wasn't a request, though it had been voiced as one, and she didn't wait for his reply before getting up and walking into the bathroom.

Ten minutes later she was back in the bedroom, washed, dressed in the jeans and tee shirt she had arrived here wearing that same morning. She was in the process of tying back her hair when Raschid stepped into the room.

She glanced at him then away again. But the glance had clung long enough to notice that he had changed too, and was now wearing one of his razor-sharp business suits. She also had time to note an unusual wariness in the way he was studying her—which she gained a nasty kind of satisfaction from seeing, because it meant that he wasn't quite so sure of her any more.

'Your mother has gone,' he informed her.

That didn't surprise Evie. Her mother was going to need time to come to terms with this next dreadful scandal that was about to fall on their seemingly beleaguered family.

'Asim tells me you have requested a taxi,' he said next. 'Why?'

'So I can leave here,' she coolly replied. 'What else?'

'Where do you intend to go?'

'Home, to Westhaven, probably,' she said. 'To hide away there as dreaded black sheep do when they're in deep trouble.'

Her sarcasm was acute; his sigh revealed his impatience with it. 'Don't deride yourself like that,' he snapped.

'Why not?' she countered. 'It's the truth after all—or at least it is the truth as everyone else is going to see it once this mess gets out.'

'Don't be foolish!' he rasped. 'You are overwrought and overreacting! Once we marry no one will give a damn when or why our baby was conceived!'

Oh, very tactful, Evie thought acidly. 'I think I've said

this to you before,' she flashed back at him. 'But this time I mean it—I wouldn't marry you now if you came gift-wrapped in rubies! I would never be able to live with what you were secretly thinking about me, you see!'

'I do not suspect you of getting pregnant deliberately!' he ground out angrily.

Evie didn't answer, but her cynical expression said a lot as her trembling fingers struggled to capture the final strands of gold hair that had escaped the ribbon she had tied the rest in.

'Okay,' he conceded with a heavy sigh. 'There was a moment—a very brief moment—when the suspicion did occur to me,' he admitted. 'What man wouldn't consider such a proposition given the circumstances of our relationship?'

'A man who knew me well enough to know I would rather die than use those kind of tactics to trap him?' Evie suggested.

The sound of his sardonic huff of laughter had Evie spinning around to stare at him. 'It seems to me that it is you who feels trapped by this situation, Evie, and that is what is really eating away at you.'

Was it? she wondered. Then heavily admitted to herself that he was most probably right. She did feel trapped in a situation that there was no way out of unless she seriously took on board the only other option open to her.

An ice-cold shudder went ripping through her; Raschid saw it and released a heavy sigh. 'Look...' he said, walking towards her. His hands came up, gripped her shoulders. 'I'm sorry if I offended you earlier. But—don't you think we have enough problems to deal with between us, without you and I fighting with each other?'

'It all feels so ugly,' she shakily confessed. 'And it's only promising to get uglier.'

She meant once his father was involved, and Raschid

instinctively understood that. 'Trust me,' he said. 'I will turn this to our advantage if it is the last thing I do.'

But at what expense? His father's pride? His country's pride? Their own wretched pride?

'Already your dear mama is feeling most unexpectedly maternal,' he added softly.

Lifting her lashes, Evie found herself looking into warm, dark, wryly amused eyes.

'Her final command to me before she left,' he explained, 'was to be sure I took precious care of her daughter or I would have her to contend with.' He smiled. 'I think we found a common ground for the first time ever when we both offended you as we did.'

'You are both more alike than you think,' Evie murmured. 'You are both arrogant, both pushy, both too full of yourself.'

'While you are nothing more than our tragically misunderstood victim; is that what you're saying?'

Evie grimaced. Put like that, she had made herself sound pathetic. 'Your own father still has to have his say in this,' she reminded him.

'He isn't some kind of ogre, Evie,' Raschid replied soberly. 'If the idea of you carrying a baby can soften your mother's attitude towards me, then there is a good chance it can soften my father's attitude to you.'

'What—so we can all play happy families together?' Her tone alone said she didn't see much hope of that ever happening.

'At least you can give him a chance before you completely condemn him.'

A chance? Oh, yes, Evie could at least give him that. But she didn't really hold out much hope for a happy ending to this.

'So, what happens next?' she asked.

Raschid removed his hands from her and straightened

his shoulders in a way that reminded Evie of those occasions she had watched him donning his official robes.

'I go home to Behran to break the news to him,' he replied.

'What—now—today?'

'Yes.' He took a quick glance at his watch. 'In the next ten minutes to be more precise.' He looked at her then, golden eyes darkened by questions.

'I really caused you a lot of problems when I didn't tell you about the baby two weeks ago, didn't I?' she murmured penitently.

His shrug said it all. 'I could have diverted my father from this course he has taken if I had known then, yes.'

'I was such a miserable coward,' Evie admitted.

'No, you were not,' he denied. 'You were shocked, you were anxious, and you were trying to do what you believed was the right thing with your brother's wedding day so close.'

'Trying to please everyone and pleasing none,' she translated with a rueful grimace.

'Well, please me now,' Raschid requested. 'And stay here while I am away. As it is, your personal possessions are on their way here from your cottage as we speak, and Asim has agreed to stay here with you. He will vet any visitors or telephone calls.'

Be her guard, in other words. 'Is he a eunuch?' she asked dryly.

'No.' His mouth twitched appreciatively at the reference. 'But I trust him with my life so I can therefore trust him with your virtue.'

'But can you trust me with his?' Evie threw back provokingly.

His answer came quick and fast—so fast she didn't even see it coming until she was locked in his arms and being utterly consumed by the kind of kiss only Raschid could issue.

'I can trust you,' he affirmed as he drew away.

And why could he sound so smugly confident about that? Because she was clinging to him, lost in him, drowning in him—as always.

But then Raschid had trouble dragging himself away from her, and it was some consolation to feel his mouth come back to hers for a hot, hungry, final kiss before he could bring himself to remove her hands from around his nape and reluctantly step away.

'I must go,' he said gently. 'My flight plan has been filed and I dare not miss my slot.'

Which meant he was intending to fly himself to Behran, Evie realised with a small shaft of alarm that had its roots in the frightening fear that, with their luck right now, anything might happen to him during the long flight.

'Take care, won't you? And call me, whenever you can!'

'I'll call,' he promised. 'And I will see you again within the week.'

Fine words, sincere words. But he didn't call her, and neither did she see him within the next two weeks.

# CHAPTER NINE

BY THEN the isolation was beginning to get to her. She hadn't dared to so much as step out of the apartment for fear of being waylaid by the press or people she did not want to see.

Oh, her mother called her up every day on the telephone. In her own way, Lucinda was trying to be supportive, but it didn't come easily to her. And really it was Evie who found herself ladling out calm reassurance to her mother when each new day went by without hearing a single thing from Raschid.

'If he lets you down in this, I'll kill him,' Lucinda vowed when a full week had gone by with no word from Raschid.

'Trust him, Mother,' Evie replied. 'I do. He loves me as much as I love him and he wants this baby. With that kind of incentive men can move mountains.'

But, as the days went by without any word from Raschid, for the first time ever Evie found herself wishing the newspapers would give her some clue as to what was going on in Behran. But they were frustratingly empty of any reference to either Sheikh Raschid or Evie Delahaye for a change. It was a matter of priorities to them. A juicy scandal had suddenly blown up involving two government ministers and the media were busy covering that.

Asim didn't help. For he too clamped up whenever Evie tried to grill him, feigning no knowledge of what Raschid was doing and advising her to be patient. But he knew more than he was admitting to, Evie was absolutely sure about that, and the fact that he wasn't prepared to speak could only mean the information filtering back to him from Behran had to be bad.

Oh, he tried his very best to make the wait bearable. In fact, she and Asim became quite close friends during those two wretched weeks. He had duties to attend to at the Behran Embassy for part of each day, but otherwise he devoted his time exclusively to her.

They walked together each morning on the roof garden attached to the apartment. And in the evenings he encouraged Evie to reacquaint herself with the game of chess—something she had played often with her father before he'd been tragically killed in a horse-riding accident when she was only ten years old.

Her arm healed quickly under Asim's care. He was a good man, a kind man, a pleasant companion, and it was during those two weeks that she began to understand why Raschid kept him close by all the time.

He also talked freely and proudly about his country and all of the changes that had been made during the last twenty years. Life in Behran, she discovered, was not as totalitarian as she had believed it to be. The women were not kept hidden behind locked doors. It was no longer compulsory for them to cover themselves when they ventured out in public. Education was compulsory for both sexes, and women were beginning to find a place for themselves in all aspects of the working society.

Only a very small section of the people wanted to keep things as they used to be, he'd told her. Most people saw the advantages in moving forward with the rest of the world rather than trying to pull against it.

But the most curious point of all she learned from Asim during these talks they shared was that all of the changes made in Behran had been effected through Raschid's father, which made his old-fashioned attitude towards marriage all the more confusing.

But then, religion did that—divided and fragmented a

human race that should be drawing closer together. Religion, colour, social tradition. Her own mother was guilty of discrimination in all three areas, so why should Evie expect Raschid's father to feel any different?

And Raschid's father did not feel different—as Evie found out for herself soon enough.

His feelings were made known to her via his personal envoy towards the end of the second week of her enforced isolation.

Asim was out attending to his duties as was his habit during the middle part of the day. Evie hadn't been feeling too well that morning—sickly and aching as if she might be going to come down with a bug.

'You are unwell, Miss Delahaye?' he'd enquired when she'd declined their usual walk on the roof garden before he'd left her.

Evie had just sent him a rueful look. 'You're the doctor,' she'd said dryly. 'You tell me why I feel sick all the time.'

Asim had grimaced his understanding of her condition, and left her lounging on one of the living-room sofas, apparently content to read a book, which she did, in a half-hearted kind of way—until the sound of steps in the hallway brought her jackknifing to her feet.

Since no one else but Asim had access to the apartment, and he wasn't due back for ages yet, she thought it was Raschid returning at last. So her eager expression reflected that assumption as the living-room door swung firmly inwards—only to cloud in confusion when two complete strangers stepped boldly into the room.

Two Arabs, to be precise, dressed in smart western suits and looking about as innocuous as two gangsters.

'Miss Delahaye?' the taller, sharper-looking of the two enquired.

Evie's stomach muscles contracted, her shoulders straightening slightly as if in readiness to receive a dreadful blow. 'Who are you?' she demanded. 'What are you doing here?'

She was offered an obsequious bow, and Evie didn't like it. It sent an icy shiver chasing down her spine, as if the cold hand of fate had just touched her shoulder.

'My apologies for this intrusion,' the spokesman murmured politely. 'My name is Jamal Al Kareem. I am come bearing messages for you from Crown Prince Hashim,' he explained.

'And Prince Raschid?' Evie questioned. 'Is he not with you?'

'Prince Raschid is engaged on—official business,' she was informed. 'In our neighbouring state of Abadilah.'

Abadilah… That cold hand touched her shoulder again. Abadilah was the state Aisha's father ruled.

'Then how did you gain access to this apartment?' she asked coldly.

'As the Crown Prince's head of security I have access to all Royal residences. It is, I am afraid, a necessary evil for powerful families to take special precautions to protect themselves,' he explained, moving ever closer to her as he spoke. 'For power brings with it its own enemies, and those enemies may decide that trouble can best be served from within, so to speak.'

He came to a stop at the rear of the sofa where Evie had been sitting. In response, Evie found herself taking a defensive step backwards, something in his super-polite, very silky tone making her feel threatened. As if he was subtly informing her that she was classed as an enemy here.

'Y-you said Crown Prince Hashim sent you,' she prompted, utilising a cool aloofness in an attempt to offset whatever it was this horrible man was giving off.

Another bow—another shiver. 'The Crown Prince is most concerned about the—predicament you find yourself in at present,' the messenger confirmed. 'He wishes me to relay to you his most sincere apologies for any—distress you have been forced to endure due to his premature announcement to the media.'

'Th-thank you,' Evie said, her eyes flicking nervously to where the other man was standing by the door—half in and half out of it as if he was on alert, listening for Asim's return. 'But you may assure Crown Prince Hashim that no apology was necessary.'

'He will be most humbly grateful for your gracious understanding,' the spokesman returned courteously. 'But the Crown Prince is—disturbed that your feelings were not taken into account when he released the statement about his son's forthcoming marriage. It was—insensitive of him, as his revered son pointed out. Now he wishes to make recompense for any distress caused to yourself...'

Watching him lift a hand to his inside pocket, Evie felt the muscles in her shoulders tighten just a little bit more. What she thought he was going to withdraw from that pocket she wasn't quite sure, but what she didn't expect to see him holding out towards her was a slender slip of paper.

Wary, confused, instinctively suspicious of what was taking place here, Evie stepped forward so she could take the piece of paper, then stepped quickly back before letting her eyes drop from Jamal Al Kareem's expressionless face to check out what she was holding. And felt a sense of chilling horror slide slowly through her blood.

It was a cheque made out to the World Aid Foundation for two million pounds.

'The Crown Prince is aware of the good work you do for this particular charity,' the messenger explained while Evie just stared unblinkingly down at the cheque. 'He begs you will accept this small donation as a—gesture of atonement. And in the light of events,' Jamal Al Kareem smoothly continued, 'he feels sure you will understand the sad necessity for him to also offer you—this...'

Evie blinked, glancing up rather dazedly to find yet another offering was being held out to her. It was a business card; she could see that even before she stepped forward to take it.

But it was only as she lowered her eyes and found herself staring at the famous logo of a very exclusive private clinic right here in London that the full horror of what was really being relayed to her here finally hit her.

'The Crown Prince is, of course, confident of your continued discretion during this—delicate time,' Jamal Al Kareem silkily concluded. 'In anticipation of your understanding, he remains your most humble servant, and hopes this will put an end to the matter...'

An end to the matter—*an end to the matter*. Those few terrible words went round and round in Evie's head as she stared at that wretched business card while her two visitors made their bows and left her to it.

She didn't move, didn't breathe, didn't do anything at all as far as she was aware. She felt strange, separated from herself almost. As if she were now standing where Jamal Al Kareem had been standing and was observing from a distance someone who looked like her, staring down at the cheque and the business card she was holding in her hands with absolutely no reaction at all.

Her face was very white, her lips cold and bloodless. Her eyes were lowered so she couldn't tell what they were doing, but her chest wasn't moving, as if her heart and lungs had simply stopped functioning, effectively cutting the oxygen off from her brain so that it couldn't even attempt to think.

Because thinking meant pain—the worst kind of pain. The pain of knowing that this truly was the—end of the matter.

No hope left. No more waiting. No chance that Raschid was going to walk through that door at any moment now and tell her that everything had been sorted in their favour.

For Raschid was in Abadilah, with Aisha.

And Evie should not be standing here in his apartment.

From that very cold, distant place she seemed to have retreated into, she watched her other self open her fingers and let both the cheque and the card drop to the floor. Then that person simply turned and walked away—out into the hallway, out of the apartment and into the waiting lift. It took her downwards. She didn't even stop when the concierge called out to her sharply.

Outside, the good weather was still holding. London was baking beneath a heatwave that had most people walking around in shirt-sleeves. So she didn't look out of place in her pale blue knitted top and casual white cotton trousers as she joined the lunchtime rush taking place on the pavements.

A car followed her for a while, though she didn't know that, its two occupants pacing her progress along the embankment until she turned onto a paved walkway where a car could not go.

An hour later—maybe two—and she was still walking. It must have been instinct that eventually made her aware of where she was, because she suddenly found herself standing outside her mother's apartment.

She rang the bell, and her mother's disembodied voice sounded in the communication box.

'It's Evie,' she heard herself say. 'Can I come in?'

There was a moment's surprised silence, then the buzzer sounded to tell Evie she could open the front door now. Her mother's apartment was on the first floor. She was already standing at the flat door when Evie got there. Lucinda took one look at her daughter and went as white as a sheet.

'Oh, my God, Evie,' she gasped in shaken dismay. 'You're bleeding!'

Evie barely heard her; she was too busy fainting at her mother's feet.

\* \* \*

It was very late that same evening and Lucinda was sitting beside her daughter's hospital bed when the door suddenly swung open and Sheikh Raschid Al Kadah stepped into the room with his faithful servant crowding right behind him.

He took one look at Evie lying so still in the bed and strode urgently forward. Only to pull to a halt when Lucinda Delahaye jumped to her feet and placed herself firmly between him and her daughter.

For once, Lucinda looked less than her usual immaculate self. Her hair was untidy, silken threads of gold were tumbling around her face where they had escaped from the elegant chignon they were supposed to be contained in. She had aged decades, her usually alabaster-smooth skin scored by lines of strain.

She grimly ushered them out of the room, firmly closing the door behind her. 'How dare you people show your faces here?' she raked at them viciously.

Raschid didn't seem to hear her. His bronzed skin looked grey, his golden eyes blackened by a terrible shock. 'The baby...?'

'Oh, I suppose it would solve all your problems to hear that she's lost it!' Lucinda lashed at him.

'No!' Raschid ground out, and swayed, his face going so white that it was only as Asim reached out to take hold of him that Lucinda realised how Raschid had misunderstood her meaning.

'Well, she hasn't lost it.' She grudgingly rectified the error. 'Though how she didn't after what your henchmen did to her has to be a miracle.'

'Is there somewhere we can discuss this in privacy?' Asim quietly suggested.

The hospital corridor wasn't busy, but some of the patients had the doors to their rooms standing open. They had to be able to hear every word that was being said.

Asim still had an arm around Raschid's shoulders while

Raschid himself seemed incapable of anything except just standing there looking devastated. And for some reason that devastation utterly incensed Evie's mother.

'You want privacy?' Lucinda hissed. 'I can give you privacy,' she grimly decreed, and stalked off down the corridor with the two men following behind her.

And she was in no mood to be pleasant. Having just gone through the worst experience of her life, watching the very lifeblood seep out of her daughter, Lucinda wanted someone else's blood as recompense.

Sheikh Raschid Al Kadah's blood.

'Do you know what those two men did to her?' she demanded the moment they were shut away inside the waiting room. 'If Evie ever forgives you in this lifetime, Sheikh, then I certainly will not!'

'It was a mistake,' he muttered, still so caught up in his first impression of what Lucinda had said to him that even with her swift correction of that misunderstanding he still hadn't recovered.

'Was it also a mistake when you didn't bother to get in touch with her for two whole weeks?' Evie's mother challenged.

'I had nothing good to say,' Raschid thickly explained. 'It seemed—kinder to wait until I could relay only good news.'

'Kind?' Lucinda scorned that excuse. 'Where was the kindness in keeping her in suspense like you did? She bottles things up!' she cried. 'She always has done! I thought you knew that! You told me you loved her! You promised to take care of her!' she went on remorselessly. 'Instead she was treated like a whore by your people!'

Raschid flinched then suddenly folded into a nearby chair to bury his face in his hands.

'Lady Delahaye...' It was Asim who tried to calm the situation, his voice that soothingly diplomatic one Evie knew so well. 'We understand and accept your right to be angry. But we would sincerely appreciate it if you could explain to us what happened after Miss Delahaye left the apartment.'

As he stood there, tall and proud beside his crumpled master, Lucinda felt a sudden urge to leap on both of them. Instead she turned her back, folded her arms across her trembling body and tried at last to get a hold on herself.

'She walked out of there with nothing,' she whispered starkly. 'In shock. No money. No idea of what she was doing—' There was a pause while she swallowed several times before she could continue. 'I don't know how long she walked for but she eventually found her way to my door—*my door*!' she swung around to fling at Raschid. 'Do you realise how far that is from your apartment? And she was bleeding!' Lucinda choked out on a wretched sob. 'Bleeding and she didn't even know it!'

Lurching violently to his feet, Raschid took two tense strides towards the door then just stopped, his whole frame clenched by some powerful inner tension that held him locked right there to the spot. 'Did they touch her?' he rasped out tautly.

'Who?' Lucinda said bitterly. 'Your men?'

'They were not Sheikh Raschid's men, Lady Delahaye,' Asim denied.

'His father's men, then—what's the difference?' she flashed. 'But in answer to your question Evie didn't say they physically touched her, only that they made her see that if your father could hate her that much, then there really was no chance for the two of you.'

'And her health?' Asim enquired gently.

Tears washed across Lucinda's eyes but she blinked them away again as determinedly as Evie herself would have done. 'She lost a lot of blood,' she replied. 'But by some quirk of fate managed to hang on to her baby. Now they are prescribing bed-rest, no stress and *no* confrontations. So I would appreciate it, Sheikh Raschid, if you would respect those things.'

A warning. A threat. The English way of issuing both that was just as effective as the Arab way.

Raschid didn't answer. But he did move at last, lifting a hand to rub wearily at his eyes before turning around to face Lucinda.

It was the first time Lucinda had actually allowed herself to look at him—and at last she saw the ravages that had taken place on his face. The man looked tormented, stripped clean to the bone of his arrogance and hurting for it.

'May I see her?' he gruffly requested.

But Lucinda firmly shook her head. 'Not without Evie's agreement,' she said. 'Seeing you may upset her, and, as I just said, I won't have her upset.'

Raschid nodded his head in acknowledgement of that. 'Then I will wait until you acquire her permission,' he announced, walked back to the chair and sat down again.

He was still sitting there twelve hours later, and even hard-hearted Lucinda was beginning to feel sorry for him.

'I don't want to see him,' Evie stated stubbornly.

'But, darling!' her mother pleaded. 'He's been sitting out there throughout the whole night! Surely that deserves some consideration!'

'I said,' Evie repeated, 'I don't want to see him.'

Lucinda looked utterly bewildered. 'I never thought I would hear myself say this, Evie,' she admitted. 'But I don't think you're being fair to the man. He's distraught! It is his baby too, you know! He has a right to reassure himself that you are both okay!'

'You reassure him, then,' Evie suggested coldly. 'The doctors say I mustn't get stressed, and Raschid stresses me.'

With that, she turned her head away to stare fixedly out

of the window. It was unbelievable what the last twenty-four hours had done to her. It was as if the trauma of almost losing her baby had forced her to grow a protective shell around herself that nobody could penetrate.

It had also brought her mother crashing down from the haughty pedestal she usually sat upon. That frightening ride in an ambulance with all sirens blaring had shaken her more than she cared to admit. For a while last night she'd truly believed she was going to lose her daughter. Shocks like those focused the mind on what was really important in life.

And nothing could be more important than life itself.

By some miracle the doctors had managed to stem the bleeding and keep the baby safe, but at what cost to her daughter's sanity Lucinda wasn't really sure, because in all Evie's twenty-three years she had never known her to cut herself off from others as coldly as she was doing now.

'I thought you loved him,' she murmured. 'In the name of that love, doesn't he deserve a hearing?'

'No,' was the blunt reply.

'Evie—'

'I'm tired now,' Evie interrupted, and closed her eyes, bit deep into the inner cushion of her lower lip, and silently prayed that her mother would drop the subject!

Surprisingly she slept. She didn't even hear her mother leave the hospital room. Next time she awoke it was dark outside and a nurse was bending over her.

'You need to eat something, Miss Delahaye,' she said. 'You've gone over twenty-four hours without food and that isn't good for your baby.'

'Can I get out of bed?' she asked; she needed the bathroom badly.

But the nurse sadly shook her head. 'Not yet, I'm afraid.' Which meant that Evie had to suffer the indignity of using a bedpan.

Which also didn't help her mood when, washed by the

nurse and her hair combed and plaited, the mobile tray that held her dinner was moved across Evie's lap and the nurse said gently, 'You have a visitor. He's been waiting for hours. Will you agree to see him, for just a minute?'

Evie stared down at the bowl of soup that suddenly tasted like sawdust in her mouth when only seconds before it had tasted rather pleasantly of chicken.

'I don't think he's going to leave here until you do see him,' the nurse added. 'He arrived late last night, and hasn't left the waiting room since except to wash and change his clothes in one of the spare rooms along the corridor. Your mother has pleaded with him, his companion has pleaded with him and we have pleaded with him. He doesn't even acknowledge that we've spoken! I have never come up against such intransigence in all my life!'

Watch this space, Evie thought coldly, and went on with her soup without making a single comment. After a while the nurse sighed and left her to it. A little while later Evie curled up on her side, folded her arms protectively over her stomach, and went to sleep thinking about Raschid sitting there in the waiting room.

The next time she came awake, a grey dawn was just beginning to lighten the bedroom—and there was a man standing at the bottom of her bed, reading her medical chart.

He glanced up when she moved. 'Good morning, Miss Delahaye.' He smiled before returning his attention to whatever he was reading. 'Your child is most determined to stay exactly where he is,' he remarked lightly. 'I suspect a mixing of two sets of very stubborn genes must give him his tenacity.'

'Asim,' Evie breathed. 'What are you doing in here?'

'I am Sheikh Raschid's personal physician,' he reminded her. 'Which now means I am his child's personal physician.'

'Is that a joke?' she demanded, using her hands to slide herself up the pillows and into a sitting position.

'No joke,' Asim blandly denied. 'Where Sheikh Raschid's child goes, I go from now on— Oh, come,' he said when he saw her expression. 'We are good friends now, are we not? You do not find me too overbearing. We will get along very well together, I am certain of it.'

'And where does Raschid fit into all of this?' Evie enquired acidly.

'At this precise moment he sits exactly where he has been sitting since he arrived here two evenings ago,' Asim replied. 'Where he now awaits my report on his child's state of health.'

'But not the mother's,' Evie bitterly assumed from all of that.

'At this stage in the proceedings, the child's health depends entirely on the mother's health so of course she matters. But as for the woman,' Asim continued smoothly, 'he accepts now that he is beyond her forgiveness. Which matters little when it is clear that he will never learn to forgive himself.'

'If you're trying to play on my sympathies, Asim,' Evie sighed, reaching out for the flask of water sitting on her bedside cabinet, 'it isn't working.'

'Here,' Asim offered instantly. 'Let me do that for you.'

Taking the flask from her, he unscrewed the cap and poured some of the chilled water into a glass before handing it to her. In silence he stood beside her and watched her drink the water, took the glass from her when she had finished and smoothly replaced both glass and flask back on the cabinet.

Then he pleaded soberly, 'See him, madam. For two nights and a day he has neither slept nor eaten and I am seriously worried about him.'

'He kept me waiting for two weeks before his henchmen came to evict me.'

'They were not his henchmen.' Asim denied the charge. 'And if you force him to he will wait two weeks in that waiting room just down the corridor, I promise you.'

Evie could believe that, knowing the man as well as she did.

'Okay,' she wearily conceded, deciding that she might as well get it over with. 'I'll see him.'

'Thank you.' Asim sent her one of those bows that reminded her of Crown Prince Hashim's messengers, and she shuddered.

'He can have five minutes then you make him leave,' she added on the back of that shuddering reminder.

'As you wish.'

What Evie wished for was to never set eyes on Raschid again, but she kept that thought to herself as Asim quickly left the room now he had what he had come for.

The door opened again in seconds, and what she saw as Raschid strode into the room almost—almost caused the shell she was hiding behind to crack.

Not with sympathy but with anger, because if this man hadn't eaten or slept in two nights and a day, he was looking disgustingly well for it!

Evie felt conned.

Conned by the pristine neatness of the clothes he was wearing, by the clean-shaven smoothness of his face and the arrogance with which he stood there by the closed door studying her with absolutely no hint of remorse written anywhere on his lean dark face.

'How are you?' he enquired.

'I'm sure everyone has told you exactly how I am,' Evie replied, in no mood for pleasantries.

He nodded politely, taking the words at their face value, then strode smoothly forward to pull out and sit down on the chair beside the bed.

It was only when he came this close to her that Evie saw the slight bruising around his eyes, which showed that the man had been going without sleep—but even those bruises added to his dark brooding sensuality, she noted resentfully.

That gut-wrenching sensuality that had been catching her out from the first time that she'd ever looked at him.

In an effort to stop herself from feeling like that, Evie dragged her eyes away and slid her knees up so she could hug them loosely with her arms. Then, head lowered, mouth clamped shut, she grimly waited for him to say what he had waited around this long to say.

Yet he didn't speak. He dragged out that silence like a taut piece of string that seemed to be trying to tug her chin up so she would look at him. But Evie refused to look at him, because looking meant communicating, as they had always been able to do with just the merest clash of their eyes. And she didn't want that kind of communication with him any more.

'I won't go away just because you wish it, you know,' he murmured eventually.

'I can't deal with you right now,' she answered flatly. 'Anyone with a bit of sensitivity would have understood that and left me to myself.'

'Because you blame me for what happened?'

Yes, she blamed him. She'd felt used, ignored, abandoned and abused by the time those two men had left her alone. Raschid had promised her protection. He had promised to call her. He had vowed to make everything work for them.

'I'm sorry my father's people frightened you so badly.'

'Your father's people are also your people,' Evie reminded him. 'I don't particularly want you to differentiate between yourself and them.'

'Why not?'

Why not? she repeated grimly to herself. 'Because you are no different, and I don't want to see you as such any more.'

'Meaning?'

'Meaning, I have been shown the light,' she answered with spiked mockery. 'And will you stop throwing questions at me as if I am the one standing on trial?' she flashed. 'In case you haven't realised it yet—I am the victim here!'

'And you think I am not just as much a victim?' His wide chest heaved, lifting and falling on a tense pull of air. 'I had no idea my father could stoop so low as to pull a lousy stunt like that!' he said savagely. 'He now deeply regrets what he did,' he added, sounding so short and clipped that if she had been anyone else Evie would have read stiff reluctance to offer that information in that haughty tone.

But she wasn't anyone else. And she knew this man inside out, so she also knew what that tone of voice really meant.

Raschid was struggling to keep his real feelings about his father under tight wraps.

'He sends you his most sincere apologies—'

'He's already done that,' she clipped, her face going white when she remembered the last person who had said those words to her.

'And begs your forgiveness,' Raschid doggedly continued as if she hadn't spoken.

Evie clamped her lips together and forbore to repeat that his father had also done that before.

'He will, of course, tell you these things personally as soon as he is fit enough to leave hospital.'

That brought her eyes up and around to stare at him. 'What hospital?' she gasped.

'The one I put him in,' he replied, the words hard with a mockery that had no hint of humour. 'When he refused to accept that I intended to marry you and not Aisha,' he went on to explain, 'I abdicated my right to succession. The shock almost killed him.'

'Oh, Raschid, no,' Evie groaned, and wondered wretchedly how many people this whole horror story was going to hurt before it was done.

'Still,' he went on coolly, 'all's well that ends well, as you British like to say. My father now has a heart which beats as healthily as my own does, and he is also reconciled to the fact that I will marry where I choose to marry.'

'Not if that marriage includes me, you will not,' Evie said stiffly.

His dark head turned, and it was only as it did so that Evie realised that he too had been avoiding all eye contact between them.

But not now. Those liquid gold eyes now pierced her with a deep, dark, grim intent. 'You *will* marry me,' he proclaimed. 'I have not spent millions of pounds and too many precious days scouring the Middle East searching for a suitable substitute to take my place as Aisha's husband, nor did I almost put my own father in his grave and place at risk both you and the child you carry simply to hear you now tell me it was all for nothing!'

'Did I ask you to do all that?' Evie countered tersely.

'Yes!' he declared. 'Every time you told me you loved me, you asked me to do those things!' he rasped. 'Every time we simply look at each other, we are demanding from the other that we go to any lengths necessary to be together!'

He got up, the passion sounding in his voice reflected in the angry movement of his body as he walked across the room to stand glaring out of the window.

While Evie sat, stunned into utter silence by his vehemence.

And the worst of it was that he was right! The kind of love they had shared during the last two years had demanded that they go to any lengths to hold on to it!

But not any more, Evie thought on a shudder. Recent

events had gone too far and turned too nasty to hang on to romantic ideals that had no place in reality.

'I can learn to live without your love,' she told him huskily. 'I can even live without people's respect!' Hadn't she been doing that very successfully for two whole years now? 'But I've discovered that I cannot live with hatred.'

'My father doesn't hate you,' he sighed. 'He simply saw you as a pawn he could use in the battle he was waging with me.'

'That makes it all right, does it?' Evie flashed back bitterly.

'No,' he heavily conceded.

'And I wasn't the real pawn,' Evie added. 'My baby was.'

'Our baby,' Raschid grimly corrected.

But Evie shook her head. 'No matter how you want to cover it up, Raschid, your father wanted this baby dead. I can't forgive that. I refuse to forgive that! So as far as I am concerned for him this baby *is* dead,' she announced. 'I will not acknowledge you as his father, and he will not bear your name. I will not place his life at risk like that from anyone again.'

'And I have no say in this? Is that what you're saying?'

'I am saying,' Evie wearily asserted, 'that if you care for this child then you will do the right thing by him and forget you ever conceived him.'

He didn't say anything for a long time after that. And the silence pealed like the toll of a funeral bell while Evie waited to find out what he was going to do.

And he looked every inch the heir to a kingdom, she noted helplessly. Body straight, chin high, that lean dark aquiline profile revealing absolutely nothing when in actual fact she knew she had just cut deep into the very heart of him with those brutal words.

'So be it,' he said suddenly, turned and walked stiffly to the door.

It came as such a shock, such a terrible, terrible shock to have him concede defeat like that that it literally smashed her control to smithereens.

And her shrill cry of, 'Raschid—no!' filled the room with more agonised despair than it could accommodate.

It made him reel around in its shock-waves, dark face certainly showing emotion now as he strode back to the bed and bent over her, his skin wiped clear of any colour, golden eyes ferocious.

'I should damn well think so!' he ground out savagely. 'I am your other half—don't you dare discard me like that again!'

Her arms were already clutching at his shoulders, his sliding beneath her so he could scoop her out of the bed.

'Now we talk sense,' he gritted, sitting down on the bed with her then, using hard fingers to angle her face so she could see the power of his fury. 'For if you think I have risked so much only to concede surrender to your sudden cowardice, then you don't know me as well as you ought to do by now!'

'You set me up!' she sobbed out accusingly. 'I am supposed to avoid that kind of stress!'

'Your stress,' he said angrily, 'was there because you were playing the ice-princess to the hilt again!'

His chest heaved on a taut rasp of air; Evie clutched all the harder at him. 'What your father did was unforgivable!' she choked.

'Then don't forgive him!' he declared with a shrug that completely dismissed the problem. 'But you *will* marry me, Evie,' he grimly ordained. 'Proudly and openly. We will bring up our child together and he *will* bear my name!'

# CHAPTER TEN

'YOU look stunning, Evie,' her brother murmured huskily. 'Raschid is a very, very lucky man.'

Is he?

Standing there gazing at herself in the mirror, Evie wondered if Raschid *was* feeling lucky to be marrying her today.

Oh, he was quick to say all the right things to pronounce his good fortune. No one but no one could deny that Sheikh Raschid Al Kadah had been very vocal about his good luck when he'd announced his forthcoming marriage to Evangeline Delahaye to the world's press three weeks ago.

But did he *feel* lucky, when there was so much he was placing at risk by marrying her?

And, more to the point, did she feel lucky? Just because, three weeks ago in that hospital bed, she had finally come to terms with the knowledge that she couldn't let Raschid go no matter what that decision was going to mean to both of them, it did not automatically follow that all the concerns she had been struggling with then had melted away.

And as she stood here now, in her old bedroom at Westhaven, alone with her brother because the rest of her family were already making their way to the registry office where she was to marry Raschid in less than an hour's time, it was those concerns that came back to haunt her.

Like the worrying ring of tight security Raschid had thrown around Westhaven when it was decided that she would come here to convalesce until they married.

Funny really, she mused, but having been with Raschid for two years and having always been aware that he was an exceedingly wealthy man in his own right, she had never known him make such a dramatic show of that wealth—until they'd come to Westhaven.

But that wealth had certainly been put on show in the very high-profile cordon that secured both the grounds and the property. Even Julian had found it necessary to prove his identity before he could gain access to his own home!

The curious press loved it; her mother serenely ignored it. Evie, on the other hand, was horrified by it.

'Is there something going on that you aren't telling?' she'd demanded of Raschid when he'd come down to Westhaven to join them for dinner one evening. 'Am I still at risk—is that what all this security is for?'

'No,' he'd denied. 'But I learn my lessons the first time they are taught to me, and by leaving only Asim to take care of you at my apartment I devalued your importance to me in the eyes of those who gauge worth by the strength of its protection.'

'The Arab mentality, you mean.'

'If you wish to call it that,' he'd conceded, refusing to take up the provoking derision pitched into the remark. 'But it is an impression that has now been rectified. No one will ever dare to approach you again in threat.'

'Does that mean I have my eunuch at last, sneaking up to guard my bedroom door every night after I've retired?' Again the remark had been sharp with acid.

'Quite obsessed with this eunuch thing, aren't you?' he'd drawled, a sleek black eyebrow arching in amused mockery at that suggestion. 'Could it be you have been weaving secret fantasies in your lonely bed at night? Maybe as a punishment to me because I refuse to share it?'

His determined abstinence in this area of their lives was just another form of protection he imposed on her that Evie found worrying. In all their two years he had never been able to resist her—she only had to remember that brief episode in her bedroom at Beverley Castle to prove that point!

But now, suddenly, Raschid rarely even laid a finger on her. Why? What could he possibly hope to gain by his abstinence now, when the damage of their loving had already been done with the conception of their baby?

He had, until now, avoided the question whenever she had challenged him with it. And it was just another worry she was having to contend with as she stood here staring at herself in the mirror.

'If you were me, Julian,' she burst out suddenly, spinning round to look anxiously at her beautifully tanned brother who had not long been back home from his month-long honeymoon sailing round the Caribbean, 'would you be marrying yourself to an Arab who lives in a Muslim state?'

'I thought true love could conquer all,' he replied with a teasing grin.

But Evie was in no mood to be teased. 'His family don't want me to be his wife,' she explained tautly. 'His people don't want me! For all I know, I may be walking myself straight into purdah!'

'Or simply suffering from a bad case of wedding nerves,' Julian suggested. 'Oh, come on, Evie!' he sighed. 'Since everyone knows exactly what Raschid feels for you, I can't see purdah being much of a problem when it would most definitely necessitate him having to share it with you!'

Then why does it feel as if I'm doing the wrong thing? she asked herself tautly as she turned back to the mirror.

What she saw standing there was a woman who was anxiously attempting to respect the traditions of two completely different cultures.

Her outfit had been made for her in-house by a top designer who had been drafted in at enormous expense by Raschid and instructed to create something incomparable, and what he had come up with was both startlingly simplistic and breathtakingly effective.

The dress was really nothing more than a long and narrow tunic with a simple high neck and long loose sleeves designed very much on Middle Eastern lines. Made of a fabulously rich antique-gold silk, its only decoration was the narrow band of delicate seed-pearls sewn down the front seam and around the tiny stand-up collar.

But it was the addition of a fine gold mesh skullcap dotted with yet more seed-pearls that gave it that special touch of glamour. On the advice of the designer, Evie had left her hair loose so the long silken mass tumbled down her spine in fine gold tendrils.

'Medieval England meets mysterious East.' Christina had softly described the effect just before she'd left for the registry office with Lucinda, putting in a nutshell exactly what it was that the designer had been trying to achieve when he'd created this look for Evie.

But what would Raschid see when he looked at her? A woman who was trying just a bit too hard to bridge the gap between two cultures?

Outside a long white limousine stood gleaming in the summer sunshine that hadn't eased its grip on England for more than two months now.

'Cheer up,' Julian gently admonished her as they drove away. 'You are supposed to be going to your wedding, not your funeral.'

Too true, Evie thought, but still couldn't shake off the chilling feeling that a dark presence was casting its shadow over the car as they drove towards Hertford.

A shadow which had a definite shape to it—Raschid's father. His family. His Arabian people. None of whom were to be present today. Oh, the reasons for that had come thick and fast enough. His father was not well enough to travel great distances. His sister could not come because one of her children had been taken ill. His Embassy people were, unfortunately, involved in important matters of state that could not be rearranged to accommodate their rushed marriage.

But Evie wasn't stupid; she could recognise denunciation when she was being fed it so blatantly.

Westhaven Town Hall was a rather elegant red-brick building that took pride of place in the old town square where a small crowd had gathered to watch—including the expected clutch of reporters.

As the car drew to a stop at the bottom of the steps, Evie could see Raschid waiting for her at the top of them. He was wearing a dark silk suit, bright white shirt and dark tie, she noted, and wondered heavily if the lack of his traditional Arab dress was just another statement she should take grim note of.

Yet her eyes clung to him as he came lightly down the steps towards the car. So tall, lean, so painfully handsome, this Arab lover of hers, she thought helplessly.

And Julian is right; I can't live without him.

After opening the limousine door for her, his eyes blazed with possessive approval as he helped her to alight. 'Beautiful,' he murmured softly.

Flash bulbs exploded, people called out. Evie plastered a social smile on her face, and let Raschid escort her to their wedding.

The civil ceremony itself was to take place in front of only a few chosen witnesses. Then they were to return to Westhaven where the rest of their guests would be waiting to watch the Christian blessing Raschid had arranged to take place there.

There was to be a Muslim blessing, too, but not here in England, and not until Raschid's father was well enough to attend it.

Or when he was ready to accept Evie as his son's wife, she suspected was the truth.

Her mother, Christina and Asim were waiting for them

inside the foyer. At least Asim was wearing traditional Arab robes, Evie noted wryly.

The service was short, over almost before it had begun. Evie stood beside Raschid and repeated her vows in a frail voice that had their few witnesses straining to hear them. Raschid's voice was stronger, but slightly constricted, as if he was finding this more of a strain than he had expected it to be.

Evie felt the ring slide on to her finger, looked down to see a band of delicate gold twining around the Al Kadah family crest.

Did this ring make her one of them now? she wondered.

'You may now kiss the bride, sir.'

Kiss the bride...

Like an automaton, Evie turned towards Raschid as he turned towards her. Lavender eyes clashed with gold. It was like free-falling into a vat of hot honey, and for several long seconds she wasn't aware of anything but this man and the power he had over her.

He didn't move—didn't attempt to claim his kiss, but just stood there looking down at her with his darkly tanned face cast into disturbingly sombre lines.

The tension grew. Evie's heart began to stutter, her parted lips trembling slightly as they waited for that kiss.

What was wrong with him? Did looking down into this face that bore no resemblance to his own people make him suddenly realise what he was actually putting at risk by joining himself to her?

By now the breathless tension was beginning to envelop everyone. No one moved, no one spoke; all eyes were fixed intently on them. Her skin began to shimmer, long lashes flickering as her eyes anxiously asked him a question.

Raschid murmured something soft in his own language—a plea to Allah, Evie thought it was. Then she felt his hand searching for and taking hold of her hand—felt the tremor in his long fingers as he drew that captured hand up between their two bodies.

His dark lashes fell over liquid gold eyes as he looked down at the crested ring adorning her finger. Then he kissed it gently and lifted his eyes back to Evie's again.

'Kismet,' he said, that was all.

Kismet. The will of Allah. Their destiny.

Evie's heart swelled to bursting. And at last she smiled. In the next moment his arms were banding around her and he was claiming his kiss.

Outside the registry office, the air had suddenly developed a crystal clarity to it that totally outshone the dark shadow of before. Flash bulbs popped again, people called out to them. Evie smiled for the cameras, serenely ignored the questions and let her new husband lead her down to the waiting limousine, which would take them back to Westhaven.

Raschid maintained a grip on her hand as the car sped them away. Evie turned to smile at him, but he didn't smile back. 'You look utterly, soul-destroyingly lovely,' he murmured huskily. 'But for a while back there you also looked heart-breakingly sad.'

'Maybe I was having second thoughts,' she said teasingly.

'Were you?' It was a serious question.

Well, Evie asked herself, was I really having second thoughts about marrying this man?

'Kismet.' She smiled. The word really did seem to say it all for both of them.

He nodded in understanding and dropped the subject to lean over and kiss her instead. But he wasn't fooled. Evie knew that he was aware that she might have answered one question but she had avoided telling him why she had looked so sad.

No giant white canopy awaited them at Westhaven, no brass band—no hundreds and hundreds of guests. Just a few close friends, a clutch of close relatives—and the summer house—where the local vicar waited to bless their union in respect of Evie's Christian faith.

An alfresco buffet lunch had been laid out on trestle tables on the lawn in front of the house. Great-Aunt Celia was present, but she sensibly avoided actually speaking to either the bride or her groom. And Harry was there, escorting a pretty young thing that gazed doe-eyed at him. Evie spied Raschid standing talking to them at one point, and wondered curiously when mutual hostility had turned into friendship.

'I've given him some of my horses to train,' Raschid explained later when she asked him the question. 'As a consolation prize for being a good loser.'

'What an arrogant thing to say!' Evie exclaimed.

'Not really,' Raschid drawled, sending her a wry look. 'For I would not have handled losing you to him as honourably as he has handled losing you to me.'

'Why?' she asked curiously. 'What would you have done?'

The hand he had resting on her still slender waist drew her around to stand in front of him. 'Guess,' he whispered.

'I think we are talking of locked doors and eunuchs again,' Evie pondered sagely.

'Preceded by kidnap, of course,' Raschid added. 'Which is exactly what I am about to do to you right now…'

As he spoke a helicopter came swooping low around the side of the house, gleaming white against the summer-blue sky and forcing the women to clutch at their hats as its rotor blades churned up the air around all of them.

It set itself down on the lawn several hundred feet away. 'Our transport away from here,' Raschid announced.

'I'll go and get changed…'

'No need.' Raschid stopped her by capturing her hand. 'You look perfect as you are. Come—say your goodbyes quickly. We are working to a very tight schedule.'

'I wish you would tell me where we are going,' Evie complained. 'I may have packed all the wrong things!'

He didn't answer, his attention already diverting to Evie's mother who was coming towards them and looking tearful.

She hugged Evie tightly. 'Look after yourself,' she said. It still amazed Evie how tactile her mother had become since she'd witnessed her daughter's near-death experience. But a bit of the old Lucinda appeared when she turned towards Raschid. 'I suppose you're expecting a motherly hug too, now,' she remarked coolly.

'Not unless it is genuinely offered,' he threw back.

Lucinda's eyes flashed, with irritation or appreciation, Evie wasn't entirely sure. But the curt, 'Just you take precious care of her!' was issued alongside a blow-softening kiss brushed against one of Raschid's lean cheeks.

'I think she is reluctantly beginning to like me,' Raschid confided as they settled into the helicopter.

Shame the same could not be said of his own family's feelings towards her, Evie thought—and just like that she felt her mood flip over from light to heavy.

He noticed, this sharp-eyed Arab of hers. 'What's wrong?' he demanded. 'What did I just say to cause you to look like that?'

'Nothing.' She found a smile from somewhere that only just made it. 'I'm tired, that's all—missing the nap Asim daily forces upon me.'

Asim was sitting up front with the pilot. Evie wasn't surprised to find he was coming with them. Everywhere Evie went these days, Asim was right there with her. He hadn't been bluffing when he'd told her that this child she was carrying was now his responsibility.

'Then as soon as we board the plane that is exactly what you will do,' Raschid ordained.

They transferred to one of the Al Kadah personal jets at a private airfield not many minutes away from

Westhaven. The moment they were up in the air, Raschid released them both from their seat belts and pulled Evie to her feet.

'Time for the lady's rest,' he explained, drawing her along the luxury main cabin and in through a door that turned out to be a fully equipped bedroom.

'Oh, very decadent,' Evie teased, looking curiously around her as Raschid moved over to the double bed that dominated the cabin, complete with passion-purple silk sheets and mounds of richly coloured silk pillows.

Picking something up from the bed, he tossed it negligently over his shoulder. It was a short silk nightdress in a very sensual dark red colour.

'Turn around,' he commanded, ignoring the taunt. 'So I can release you from this exquisite creation.'

Evie did as he bade her. 'I feel I must inform you that as a full-blooded Arab I am feeling very cheated at this precise moment,' he said lightly as his deft fingers dealt with the long zip that ran down the length of her spine. 'I was expecting those seed-pearls decorating your front to be my one hundred and one buttons—as is the traditional way Arab women drive their new husbands crazy while they are forced to unwrap their prize inch by painful inch.'

'But you don't want what's beneath this gown,' Evie pointed out. 'So why bother to mention it?'

'Is that what you really think?'

The dress was eased away from her shoulders, and allowed to slither to the floor. Evie reached up to pull off the skullcap while kicking off her white satin slip-ons at the same time. She felt Raschid's fingers at the clasp of her smooth satin bra, and quivered slightly as his warm flesh touched her flesh.

'Yes,' she said.

She heard his soft laugh as he bent down to deal with the only piece of clothing she had left. Seconds later, she was naked, and his hands were gently clasping her slender hip bones. The brush of his mouth against the curving cheeks of her bottom made her spine arch in stinging response.

'Liar,' he drawled. 'You know I adore every single inch of this delectable body.'

Then he was turning her to face him, his hands still holding her there in front of him while he continued to squat at her feet. In a slow, slow, agonisingly sensual drift of his heavy eyelids, he inspected her from bare toes upwards.

Her legs turned to liquid, her thighs began to burn, that hidden place between them pulsing out its needy message. He inspected the pale-skinned flatness of her stomach where their baby was not yet making its presence felt, drifted those hooded eyes up over her rib-cage to her breasts where a new firm fullness was most definitely evident.

'Every inch,' Raschid repeated huskily.

Evie dragged in a constricted breath of air, her hand snaking up to cup his lean cheek so that she could make him look at her. His eyes changed colour, darkening on a swirling tempest of craving. Her thumb moved, brushing across his lips to gently part them. The moist inner heat lining the recess of his mouth drew powerfully on some inner heat of her own that had her folding to her knees in front of him.

'I don't really need to rest, you know,' she told him softly. 'But I do need you.'

'Ah...' he sighed sorrowfully. 'But—'

Evie smothered the 'but'. She crushed it right back into his mouth with the hungry press of her own. What was absolutely glorifying was the fact that he didn't attempt to fight her. He let her deepen that kiss to a bone-melting intimacy that made her feel alive and happy for the first time in weeks.

He still held her hips tightly between his two hands;

Evie used her own hands to begin urgently dealing with his clothes. As far as she was concerned, he was wearing too many; impatient fingers tossed the nightdress to one side then began pushing his jacket from his shoulders before yanking at his tie.

In all their two years she had never longed for him as much as she was longing for him right now, and it showed in the small growl of triumph she made against his mouth as the tie came free.

Shirt buttons then began popping without a care to how they came free. He wasn't helping her—which only incited her urgency. The shirt came to rest around his elbows with his jacket, trapped there by the hands he still had clamped to her hip bones.

Evie didn't care; she had warm, tight skin to touch at last, and a wonderful hair-roughened breastplate to reacquaint herself with. Her mouth wrenched itself away from his so it could go and taste that newly exposed flesh.

On a tormented groan, Raschid suddenly burst into action. He freed his arms from his trailing clothes, reached for her, pulling her hard against him, his hot mouth homing in on tight, tingling nipples that set her whole body singing.

How long had it been since they'd been together like this? Five weeks?

It showed in the violence of their breathing, in the urgency with which they began to devour each other. He sucked so hard on one of her nipples that she actually whimpered—then laughed because she had missed his mouth on her like this so very badly.

Breathing gone haywire, bodies hot, emotions locked into a raging frenzy. When he dragged himself to his feet, Evie rose up with him, her arms wrapped tightly around his neck.

His mouth found hers again; she clung to him, her breasts pressing against him in open provocation. But when she dropped her hands to the waistband of his trousers his reaction was so unexpected that it thoroughly stunned her. Picking her up in his arms, Raschid turned and dumped her on to the bed.

'No!' he ground out, jerked right away from her, then spun on his heel to bend and snatch up the discarded nightdress, which he tossed at her before bending to snatch up his shirt.

'Wh-what do you mean—no?' she gasped, barely able to believe he really meant what he was implying here!

'I'm sorry,' he muttered. 'I didn't mean to become so carried away. But we must not,' he added tautly. 'I made a vow...'

'A vow?' Evie repeated shrilly, beginning to shake all over in reaction. 'What kind of vow?'

'Cover yourself,' he commanded roughly.

Having recently devoured her with his eyes, he was now looking anywhere but at her, his dark face a mask of bone-gripping tension. Evie knew that look. He was hurting, and at this precise moment she was glad he was hurting!

'What kind of vow?' she angrily insisted.

'A vow to Allah,' he confessed. 'That I would treat you with respect.'

'I've got news for you, Raschid,' Evie informed him, grimly dragging the nightdress over her trembling flesh. 'This doesn't feel like respect, it feels like rejection!'

He winced as if she'd hit him, but it didn't stop that wonderful chest Evie had just eagerly exposed for herself from disappearing behind snowy white linen.

'That is because you misunderstand my motive,' he explained, bending to retrieve his jacket and his tie next. 'For too long I have undervalued your importance to me. It is a sin I am determined to put right.'

'What sin?' she demanded bewilderedly. 'The sin of wanting to make love to me?' She sounded so damned offended that his mask of a face seemed to turn to iron.

Yet he nodded his dark head in sombre confirmation. 'And the sinful lack of understanding as to what our relationship was doing to your pride, your self-esteem and your reputation.'

'Is this explanation supposed to make me feel better?'

'It will, when I've finished,' he said, dragging his jacket back on.

He didn't look so elegant now, Evie noted caustically, with half the buttons on his precious shirt missing! 'Then by all means please go on!' she invited. 'For I find myself completely enthralled by all of this—humility!'

He muttered something she didn't catch—an Arab curse aimed at sarcastic females, she suspected.

'I exposed you to mockery, humiliation and danger,' he nonetheless continued. 'I stood by and watched your own family shun you at your brother's wedding. I witnessed the whole party freeze in horror when you caught Christina's bridal bouquet! I then watched you stand alone by a moonlit lake and toss those damn flowers into the water as if you were tossing away all hope for you and me!' His chest heaved on an angry rasp of air.

'Yet, seeing all of this,' he grimly went on, 'knowing exactly how wretched you must have been feeling, I still responded badly to your news about the baby! How you could bring yourself to speak to me after that performance,' he concluded gruffly, 'I will never comprehend!'

Evie said nothing—what could she say? He was only telling it as it was, after all. She *had* been tossing away hope with those flowers. He *had* reacted badly about the baby.

'You didn't even carry a bouquet to our wedding,' he then inserted huskily. 'Do you think I did not see the significance in that omission? I have this dreadful suspicion that if you ever hold another flower in your hand you are always going to see that cursedly doomed bouquet in its stead!'

He was probably right, so Evie didn't argue the point with him. 'I still don't see what any of this has to do with you and I making love now that we are married.'

'I made a vow to Allah,' he said, bringing the whole unbelievable conversation reeling back to where it had begun. 'While I waited out my vigil in that hospital waiting room, I promised Him that if He gave me a final chance with you I would never, ever undervalue your worth to me again. And since sex is all I ever gave to you before,' he finally concluded, 'then sex will now await its pleasure, until I have proved to you that you mean more to me than just a source of physical gratification.'

And that was what this was really all about? He'd made some silly vow to Allah while sitting in a hospital waiting room turning himself inside out with guilt and worry?

'In case it has escaped your notice,' Evie dryly mocked, 'I tended to use you in exactly the same way.'

To her surprise, he laughed one of those warm, husky, very male laughs that eased some of the tension out of him.

'Then take pity on me,' he pleaded, turning rueful eyes on her. 'And make this penance I have set myself easier to bear by lusting after me when I cannot see you doing it.'

Evie relaxed back into the pillows, no longer angry, but studying him thoughtfully. 'You won't be placing the baby at risk by making love to me, you know,' she said. 'If that's what this is really all about.'

'It isn't,' he denied.

'I asked the doctor last week when I went for my check-up,' she persisted regardless. 'And he assured me that physical intimacy would not be a problem.'

He wasn't blind; he could see exactly what her lavender eyes were offering him. 'The world is full of practised sirens,' he remarked wearily. 'But why did I have to marry myself to one?'

'Kismet,' Evie said, her eyes openly provoking him now.

'Purdah is beginning to take on a whole new appeal where you are concerned,' he warned. Then, on a sigh, he came to sit down beside her, and leant down to softly kiss her cheek. 'Why don't you put me out of my misery and go to sleep?' he suggested.

'I can't convince you to change your mind and join me?' A delicate finger came up to gently play with his mouth.

'No.'

'Even though this is my wedding day and I am feeling terribly neglected?' The finger moved to his jawline, and began trailing downwards to where the whorls of crisp dark hair were showing above the gap in his open shirt. 'I promise not to try to seduce you.'

'You are seducing me already.' He utterly derided that promise, pointedly removed the trailing finger, and got to his feet again.

'How can you make a pact with Allah about something as important to us as sex?' Evie cried, losing all patience.

'Rest,' he commanded, moving back to the door.

'All right,' she snapped, sitting up again. 'I'll rest when you tell me how long this penance of yours is to last.'

For some reason the question put tension back into his shoulders. Alarm shot through her, the horrible suspicion that he was hiding something from her chilling her blood.

'Raschid...' she murmured as a sudden frightening thought struck her. 'There isn't something wrong with me or the baby that people aren't telling me, is there?'

'Of course not!' he snapped, spinning round to frown at her. 'You and the baby are perfectly healthy!' he stated tersely. 'No one has lied to you about that!'

'Then what are you hiding?'

The breath hissed from his lungs on a sigh of frustration, and for a moment, a very brief but telling moment, Evie saw indecision flash across his eyes before he turned his back on her.

'Nothing,' he said.

But it was already too late; Evie had seen that indecision, and panic was suddenly erupting inside her. Climbing off the bed, she walked towards him. Her hand was trembling as she gripped his arm. 'Don't lie to me,' she thrust at him angrily. 'Don't ever lie to me! There is something going on here that you aren't telling me, and I want to know just what it is!'

The muscles beneath her gripping fingers bunched, his lean dark profile clenching on the power of whatever it was he was trying hard to suppress here.

Evie watched and waited, his tension becoming her tension, the war he was having with himself becoming her war until the prolonged silence began to buzz like an alarm bell vibrating along tautly stretched nerve-ends.

Then he turned his head, saw her strained pallor, the anxiety that was darkening her eyes, and on a soft curse he surrendered.

'Okay,' he said, taking hold of her hand to grimly lead her back to the bed. Sitting her down there, he then looked around him for a chair and set it so that he could seat himself right in front of her. 'I was going to leave this as long as I could before telling you,' he admitted. 'But I can see that what you're thinking is possibly worse than reality. So...'

Leaning forward to take hold of her hands, he announced very gently, 'I am taking you home, Evie. To Behran...'

Behran— Evie's mind went up like a volcano, shock, horror, a bone-chilling sense of trepidation all straightening her spine on a constricted gasp of dismay.

'You have nothing to fear,' Raschid quickly assured her. 'Do you think I would be doing this if I believed it would place you in danger?'

No, she didn't think that, but it didn't alter the fact that the very idea of going to his homeland was filling her with horror.

Yet—she should have seen this coming! Why hadn't she seen it coming? She had just married this man! She was now the wife of the future ruler of Behran! She carried his child inside her—maybe the next ruler of Behran after Raschid!

'Why?' she managed to breathe out fraily.

'Because this visit is necessary,' he replied. 'To have avoided taking you home directly after our marriage would have given rise to the suggestion that I am ashamed of my western wife.'

He was talking pride here—defiance in the face of any dissension.

'Wh-what is this going to mean?' she asked, forcing the words past all the horrors that were trying to possess her. 'Will I have to face them the moment we get off the plane?'

'No.' His fingers were squeezing hers tightly, urging her to trust what he was telling her. 'We will transfer from the plane to a helicopter at the airport,' he explained, 'then fly directly to my private palace. The news will spread quickly enough that we are there together, and thereby lay to rest any suspicion that I am reluctant to bring you home. But you need see no one,' he promised. 'We will, in effect, be on our honeymoon, which will give you the chance to acquaint yourself with my way of life before we have to present ourselves officially as a couple.'

He meant to his father, though he was careful not to make the dreaded connection out loud.

Aware of his eyes still fixed intently on her, that he was tense, worried, and unsure as to how she was going to respond to this challenge he was setting before her, Evie lowered her eyes to their hands where they rested on her silk-covered lap, and tried desperately to pull her ragged senses together.

Raschid was a man of two cultures. He was used to slipping in and out of two different guises depending on which part of the world he was in. But she wasn't. In all the time they had been together it had never once occurred to him to invite her to his homeland. She hadn't even been invited to any of the functions Raschid had attended at his own embassy. For two long years she had not existed, as far as his people were concerned.

A few weeks ago they had certainly acknowledged her—by declaring her an enemy. Or, to be more precise, her baby was the enemy.

She shivered, recalling that memory, recalling too what had happened after it. Raschid felt that shiver and understood exactly what was causing it.

'Look at me, Evie!' he commanded. 'Look into my eyes and see what you always see written there!'

Blinking herself into focus, she found herself staring at strong brown fingers tightly interlaced with delicate white ones like a love knot that was too intricate to break. And there, nestling amongst this mingling of brown and white, was a gold-crested wedding band that seemed to be telling her that this was it. The moment when she finally took on board what it really meant to be joined to this very special man.

You stand proudly beside him, and boldly take them all on—or why are you here at all?

And really, she told herself, she could have no argument with it. She had married him for good or bad. If the good was in looking forward to spending the rest of her life with him, then the bad had to be where they were going to live out that life.

Then she made herself look into those dark gold, passionately glowing eyes. Made herself see what he was insisting she see. Made herself acknowledge it. I love you!

those eyes were telling her. You are my heart, my life—
my soul! I would lay down my own life before I would
let anyone get close enough to hurt you again!

'Will I have to cloak and veil myself?' she asked. 'And
make sure I walk two paces behind you?'

It took a moment—more than a moment—for what she
was actually saying here to finally sink in. But when it
came his reaction took her breath away. The husky growl
of exultation he emitted was all the warning she received
before she found herself flat on her back with him lying
on top of her.

'I knew you were brave,' he uttered proudly. 'I knew
you were the right woman for me!'

'I should really be telling you to go to hell,' she said.
'Get my own back on you for the way you refused to listen
to reason about Julian's wedding. But you like to pick your
moments, don't you?' she sighed. 'Nowhere for me to
run,' she dryly pointed out as her eyes made a rueful scan
of their present surroundings. 'Nowhere for me to—'

His mouth stopped the words of complaint with a kiss
that was both hot and possessive. But before Evie could
turn it into something much more satisfying he was, frustratingly, breaking them apart again.

'No.' He refused her yet again. Only, this time Evie was
not offended—but challenged.

'I'll break that iron will of yours,' she vowed as he made
quickly for the door. 'I will whittle away at it at every
opportunity I'm offered.'

'Part of my penance,' he accepted with a sigh. 'It will
be interesting to discover how long I can hold out.'

Or how long I can maintain this brave face, Evie mused
heavily when he had left her.

His father...

She shuddered, turning to curl into a ball on her side as

if making herself smaller would diminish the dread that name filled her with.

Did Crown Prince Hashim know they were on their way to Behran? Had Raschid told him?

She was to find out soon enough...

# CHAPTER ELEVEN

IT WAS late into the evening local time when the plane finally touched down at Behran Airport. Dressed more casually now, in a turquoise silk wrap-around skirt and long-sleeved cotton top, Evie stared out of the window at a scene that was, as with most airports, a hive of activity irrespective of the lateness of the hour.

'I didn't realise that Behran Airport was such a busy one,' she remarked to Raschid who was sitting beside her.

'It isn't—not by international standards anyway.' He frowned, dipping his dark head so that he too could glance out through the small porthole window.

In the next second he was calling sharply for Asim who came hurrying down the aisle towards them. Reverting to Arabic, Raschid shot out a couple of curt questions that had Asim ducking his covered head to peer out of the window himself before he murmured something and walked off towards the flight deck.

And Evie felt the tension begin to seep back into her system because neither man looked happy. 'What's wrong?' she asked Raschid.

'I don't know yet.' He was still frowning. Like herself he had changed just before they were due to land, only the difference between them was that he had reverted to Arab robes, and suddenly looked all the more alien for it with that black frown marring his face. 'But there is too much activity out there for this time of night.'

Perhaps not the most comforting thing to tell her, Evie mused as she glanced out of the window again. They were still taxiing towards the main airport building. It was dark, of course, but the darkness had been diminished by the excessive amount of halogen lighting that seemed to be spotlighting the plane as it moved. And beneath the lights she could see people—lots of people standing watching their arrival as if they had nothing better to do.

Asim came back, his expression more sombre than when he had walked away. He relayed some information to Raschid in Arabic that had Raschid angrily freeing himself from his seat belt and standing up.

Pushing past the other man, he strode off towards the flight deck himself.

'Be calm,' Asim told Evie soothingly when he saw her expression. 'It is nothing to worry about.'

Then why are both you and Raschid looking distinctly worried? she wanted to ask, but managed to keep the challenge to herself while her eyes remained fixed on the doorway Raschid had disappeared through.

The tension began to heighten the longer he was away. By the time he did finally reappear, the plane had come to a standstill some way off from the main building itself.

'Don't be too alarmed,' he warned, which thoroughly alarmed her. 'But my father has been interfering with my plans again.'

'Wh-why?' she said nervously. 'What has he done?'

'He has arranged a reception committee to meet us here at the plane. I'm sorry,' he sighed, coming to sit himself down beside her. 'This was not what I wanted. But—if you will just try to see it as a positive manoeuvre—in his own way he is trying to offer you a welcome.'

But you're not feeling very positive about this, Evie thought as she felt all that bravery he had attributed her earlier drain right away.

'What do I have to do?' she asked, glancing warily sideways to see what looked like a dozen people in flowing robes making determinedly for the plane.

Her stomach flipped, her legs turned to jelly. Maybe she

even trembled a little, because Raschid reached across her and slammed the shutter down over the window.

'You will be yourself,' he firmly replied. 'I ask no more of you.'

'Be myself in a cloak and veil?' she drawled suggestively, expecting him to instantly deny the challenge.

But he didn't. Instead his expression darkened perceptibly. 'I would request that you wear the gown you married me in today,' he said. 'As a sign of respect,' he quickly explained. 'For those people who have come here so late in the evening to officially greet you.'

'One being your father,' Evie murmured grimacingly.

'No,' he denied. 'My father is not quite strong enough to leave his palace. So we,' he added slowly, 'are to go to him.'

'What, now?' Evie jerked out, twisting her head to stare at him. 'Tonight?'

'It is perhaps a sensible alternative, when my father's palace is only a few minutes' drive away from here,' he said. 'Whereas my palace is still another hour's flying by helicopter away.'

But, sensible or not, Raschid was still angry at the way his plans had been outmanoeuvred; Evie could see that in the grim set of his jaw. He was also uneasy about what all of this really meant; she could see that in the frown that still pulled at his brows, and in the perturbed glitter he was trying hard to hide beneath the heavy droop of his lashes.

'What do you really think this all means?' she questioned huskily. 'And be honest with me, Raschid,' she added. 'I would rather be prepared for the worst than have it suddenly dumped on me so late that I have no time to react.'

'As I dumped this trip on you too late for you to react?' He grimaced.

'No.' Evie smiled, and to her own surprise the smile relaxed some of the tension out of her. 'Because your instincts were right and if you'd warned me that you were going to bring me here before we left England, I would probably have refused to come,' she admitted.

Seeing the smile seemed to relax him too, and he reached out to touch a gentle finger to the corner of her upturned mouth. 'I am going to take my own advice and be very positive about this,' he murmured softly to her. 'So I am going to put to you that I think my father's intentions are entirely honourable, and he is attempting here to heal the breach at the first opportunity we are handing him.'

'And you want me to do the same,' Evie concluded from that.

'Can you?'

'I can try,' she agreed. 'But I can't say I'm looking forward to any of this.'

It took only a few minutes to change back into her antique gold wedding gown. Asim found her a long white silk scarf from somewhere, which he advised her to drape loosely around her face.

Stepping back into the main cabin, she found that Raschid, too, had changed the dark blue outer robe he had been wearing for a much more dramatic black silk one trimmed with gold. And as he turned to face her she saw that a wide gold sash was now wrapped around his lean waist.

The black and gold made him look different somehow, taller, darker—disturbingly alien as he ran golden eyes still sharpened by anger over her covered head to her satin-shod feet.

'Well?' she said, smiling tightly across a tension that was beginning to make her face muscles feel very brittle. 'Do I look presentable enough for your welcoming party now, do you think?'

Those lushly fringed, heavy-lidded eyes lifted up to clash with mocking blue. They saw the anxiety hiding behind clear-cut crystal, and the strained pallor behind the creamy smoothness of her skin framed by the silk scarf.

Without saying a word he came to her, placed the tips of his long brown fingers beneath her chin to raise it—then kissed her, hard and hot, arrogantly uncaring that Asim stood by the closed exit door witnessing the embrace.

By the time he let her back up for air again, the pallor had altered to a soft flush of pink pleasure, and those cut-crystal eyes had darkened. 'Now you look delicious,' he murmured huskily, a teasing amusement suddenly dancing in his eyes. 'Quite the shyly blushing bride in fact.'

Shyly blushing bride indeed! Evie thought caustically. 'Well, whatever you say, this blushing bride is not walking two paces behind you,' she warned, taking a firm grip on one of his hands while valiantly hiding her fears behind a mask of black humour.

The sound of his deep warm burst of appreciative laughter was the last thing Evie's consciousness absorbed as she floated through the ordeal of meeting several prominent dignitaries and their wives, all smoothly introduced to her by the man whose hand her own remained glued to.

A long black limousine awaited them. It was a relief to disappear inside it. But it seemed that the ordeal was not yet over.

Sitting there beside Raschid, Evie gazed out of the car window as the car sped off towards the wire fencing that surrounded the airport complex. Big mesh gates swung open as they reached them, and without a pause the car drove smoothly out on to a tarmacadam road then turned right towards the city she could see lighting up the dark skyline in the distance.

But they hadn't gone many yards before the inky darkness on either side of them was suddenly ablaze with light. Evie sat forward, felt as she did so Raschid's increased tension as he too did the same, staring out of his own side window.

At the very same moment a loud noise erupted, startling her enough to make her gasp. The road was alight with car headlights, the noise deafening with horns being pressed as their car swept by.

Beside her, Raschid muttered something, sank back into the soft leather seat and was then oddly silent.

'What is it?' she questioned worriedly. 'Why are they doing this?'

Turning to look at him, Evie was utterly dismayed to see his face had gone strangely grey. And he seemed to be having difficulty swallowing.

'Raschid?' Concern for him had her hand reaching out to grasp one of his.

'Be at peace,' he soothed her. 'It is nothing to worry about.'

His voice was unsteady as he said the words, and if he wasn't worried then something extreme was certainly disturbing him.

'You look—hurt,' she whispered, feeling her own throat thicken in aching response to his distress.

'No,' he denied. And at last turned suspiciously moist eyes in her direction. 'They are welcoming us,' he informed her gruffly. 'They...' One long-fingered hand lifted to make an expressive gesture towards the car window. 'My people,' he extended, 'are welcoming us...'

Evie's heart flipped over, the breath seized in her breast as full understanding finally hit her. His people were welcoming them and Raschid was so moved by the gesture that he could barely contain his feelings.

'Are you okay?' she asked softly.

'Yes,' he replied, but it was very obvious that he wasn't. This had come as a real shock to him. He had not expected it and that was why it was having such a powerful effect on him.

An effect that had Evie's own eyes glazing over as she wisely said nothing more while she gave him the chance to get himself together.

My people, he had called them. My people, in the truly possessive sense of the words. My people, whom he so obviously loved and whose love and respect he had been prepared to sacrifice for her sake.

As Evie sat there beside him while they drove between the cavalcade of lights and sounding horns that lined their route as far as the eyes could see, she finally began to understand what Raschid's Kismet was doing for them here.

And she was humbled. Humbled by its force and by the man beside her who'd had the courage to reach out and grasp his own personal Kismet no matter what the cost might be.

For she hadn't been the brave one here, not really. All she'd done was follow where her heart led her, but Raschid possessed two hearts, one of which had been in conflict with the other since the day he'd set eyes upon her. He must have always known that one day he was going to have to risk breaking one of those hearts. The heart that belonged here with his people, or the heart that belonged to Evie.

What he had done was place his trust in Kismet.

And this was his reward—not hers.

She was so very, very humbled by that.

'I love you,' she told him softly, although why she did she didn't really know now; those words seemed so inadequate when set against all of this.

Yet he turned and smiled at her, and that smile was so warm and dark and soul-stirringly tender that she knew the words were not inadequate to him.

'Look,' he said then, drawing her attention back to her own window. 'My father's palace,' he said.

Out there, beyond the glaring headlights, Evie found

herself staring at a gold-lit stone building standing on its own raised piece of desert with a star-studded black velvet sky as its backcloth.

Surrounded on all sides by what looked like a twenty-foot-high boundary wall, complete with domed lookout towers on each of its four corners, it was as if the whole scene had leapt straight out of an Arabian nights picture book she remembered having as a child.

Awesome, mysterious, breathtakingly dramatic.

Two huge wooden gates cut into the wall swung inwards as they approached them. As tall as the wall itself, they were a commanding sight on their own, but when Evie realised that they guarded an entrance that was as deep as it was tall she began to understand what true awe was.

Inside was a vast courtyard, softly lit by concealed lighting that sparkled against fine sprinkles of water spouting from ornamental statues set within the exotic shrubs that grew in abundance on either side of the driveway.

The entrance to the house was a flower-hung archway of pure white marble. Clear blue light was seeping out from beyond it, and as the car stopped by a pebbled area that covered the last ten feet or so to the entrance Evie saw a woman step out from beneath the archway.

She was beautiful, dark-haired and slender but exquisitely rounded, and was wearing a long dark red silk dress that shimmered as she moved.

'Ranya,' Raschid murmured softly, and climbed out of the car to stride quickly towards her, too eager to greet his sister to remember his usually impeccable manners.

It was therefore left to Asim, who had travelled in the front of the car with them, to open Evie's door and help her to alight.

Despite the fact that the hour was so late, the air was hot and very humid, and redolent with the fragrance of gardenia, oleander and heavily scented jasmine—all overlaid by a seductive aroma of some exotic spice Evie

couldn't quite capture. Music was playing somewhere—
that distinctly Arabian sound that was so evocative of her
surroundings.

Strange, alien, yet so disturbingly seductive it made her
toes tingle and her heart thump heavily in her chest. Or
maybe those feelings had more to do with the way Raschid
and Ranya were embracing each other with an affection
that reminded her of herself and Julian.

And why should they not? she asked herself. They were
brother and sister—true brother and sister, born to the
same mother and the only children of a man who, on the
distinction alone of being a rich Arab Prince, should have
produced a hundred children to a hundred different wives.

Yet he had not. Crown Prince Hashim Al Kadah had
only ever taken one wife. When she'd passed away while
his children were still young, he hadn't bothered to replace
her.

But then, she mused as she stood there by the car waiting to be remembered, if his wife had looked anything like
his daughter Ranya, then it was perhaps understandable
why the Crown Prince had never found another woman
who could take his wife's place.

It was Ranya who noticed Evie standing there, but as
she went to move around her brother with the intention of
coming forward Raschid stopped her with a question.
Pausing, Ranya answered him, and there followed a hurried discussion in soft-voiced Arabic that to Evie, witnessing their body language, verged on the heated.

Then Ranya sighed, touched her brother's arm with
what Evie read as a gesture of sympathy, before firmly
stepping around him to walk towards Evie.

After witnessing the heat in their altercation, Evie
wasn't quite sure how she should greet this new sister-in-
law of hers—with open warmth or defensive coolness? she
pondered.

But the lovely creature made the decision easy. 'At last

we meet.' Her embrace was both warm and welcoming, touching her lips to each of Evie's cheeks. 'I am Ranya, Raschid's beloved sister, in case he has never bothered to mention me,' she said with a teasing smile that literally stopped Evie's breath because it was so like the smile her brother could use on occasion. 'May I call you Evie, as Raschid does?' she requested while gently urging Evie into movement.

The house waited; Evie wasn't at all sure, now that she had come this far, that she wanted to enter it. As she drew level with Raschid, she noticed his tension was back again. 'What now?' she whispered tautly.

He didn't answer; instead he reached for her hand then turned grimly to the archway. In silence they walked into his father's home, where the hot desert air instantly tempered to a delicious coolness.

Evie found herself standing in a vast reception hallway the likes of which she had only ever seen in history books. It was as big as a moderate theatre hall, with a high domed roof elaborately decorated with pale blue and gold mosaic tilework. The floor beneath her feet was white marble, the eggshell-blue painted walls broken by a dozen archways that led off into what she suspected was a maze of corridors. Above each arch, diamond-shaped grilles covered what Evie presumed were the Arabian equivalent of interior windows where people could look down unseen on the hallway beneath.

'This is lovely,' Evie breathed softly.

Other than giving a brief smile of acknowledgement, Raschid seemed barely to hear her; his hand touched her arm to indicate which corridor he wanted to take. And the further they went down that corridor, the tenser he became.

'Raschid—what is it?' she asked anxiously, very conscious of his sister walking with them.

This time he didn't even attempt to dissemble. Instead he stopped walking suddenly, turned to take her by the shoulders then pushed her up against the corridor wall so he could stand right over her while his sister paused several delicate yards away.

'We have yet another ceremony to go through tonight,' he announced, sounding clipped and grim and beginning to look just a little jaded around the edges. 'Again, my father has arranged this. And again I find I am in no position to argue with his decree.'

'A marriage ceremony, you mean?' she asked.

'Of course.' He grimaced. 'What else? Do you think you are up to it?'

Like him, Evie didn't think she was being given very much choice in the matter. 'What do I have to do?' she asked heavily.

'Nothing but stand beside me and repeat the vows you will be asked to say in Arabic. And I pray to Allah that then we will be allowed to do what we came here to do and be private,' he sighed out sardonically.

'But you don't hold out much hope,' Evie dryly assumed from all of that.

'No,' he confessed. 'I do not.'

'Raschid—' Ranya's voice softly interrupted them. 'We really must go now…'

Another sigh, then his mouth clamped into a flat line of grim perseverance. 'Come,' he said, taking hold of Evie's hand again. 'Let's get it over with.'

Not the most diplomatic thing to say to his bride. But then, Evie mused as they began walking along that long corridor again, how many times did he have to marry this wretched bride before he could be allowed to feel married?

They stopped at a door. Raschid seemed to need a moment to compose himself for what was to come next, and his fresh bout of tension became Evie's tension as, with a perceptible straightening of his broad shoulders, his fingers tightened around Evie's hand and his other hand reached out to open the door.

What followed became lost in the realms of a dream-like sense of unreality. The room was dark—lit only by wall-mounted candles that gave off too little light for her to see very much of what was around her.

She was vaguely aware of people standing in the dimness, vaguely aware of their curious scrutiny as Raschid led her forward. The ceremony was short—shorter than she had expected. Beside her, Raschid quietly translated every word into English for her, before she was then required to repeat them in Arabic. And through it all she kept her body in touch with his body, needing to feel the security of his presence in this alien place with its alien service and its alien sounds and scents and language.

When it was over, Raschid's attention was claimed almost instantly. As he turned to speak to the several men who had come up to him, Ranya appeared at Evie's side.

'Come,' she said quietly. 'We must go this way...'

'But—' Evie did not want to leave Raschid; glancing around her, her eyes caught sight of him standing several feet away. Her hand went out, anxious to catch his attention, but even as she did so the group of men closed in around him, and Ranya's hand on her arm was firmly guiding her away through a door that led into frighteningly unfamiliar territory.

Not a corridor, but another dimly lit room which then led through to another and another... All were richly furnished, all wore the stamp of eastern luxury. At a fourth door, Ranya paused and turned what Evie presumed was supposed to be a reassuring smile on her before she was knocking on the door.

Someone called out in Arabic. A man's voice. A sudden sense of dreadful foreboding shot like a steel rod along her spine. Ranya opened the door and stepped inside with Evie in tow.

After the eastern splendour of all the rooms they had passed through, Evie was expecting to find herself stepping into yet more of the same. She was therefore surprised to find herself standing in a big but definitely old-fashioned library that could have been transported right out of Victorian England.

It was all oak panelling lined with shelves upon shelves of leather-bound books. Richly coloured Persian rugs covered the polished wood floor and there was even a large polished oak fire surround with a log fire burning in the grate—although it did so behind a shield of heat-reflective glass.

The chairs and sofas were of old English dark red velvet, and several huge desks were groaning under the weight of the books and papers scattered across them.

And it all felt so very strange—as if she had just walked into her grandfather's study on one of those duty visits she used to make to his home with her mother when she was a child.

Her grandfather had been a stern, sombre man who'd married very late in life and never seemed to quite understand how he had produced someone as beautiful and sophisticated as Lucinda.

But this wasn't England, this was not her grandfather's Victorian study, she reminded herself. This was Behran, and the man who was at this precise moment carefully pushing himself up from one of the wing-backed chairs was most definitely not her grandfather.

'I bring Raschid's wife to you as requested, Father,' Ranya quietly announced.

And it was at that precise moment that Evie froze.

Eyes cold and fixed, the breath catching in her throat, Evie found herself staring at the tall and lean figure of— the enemy.

An enemy that could be no other person than Raschid's father, simply because looking at him was like taking a glimpse into the future and seeing exactly how Raschid was going to look thirty years from now.

Even the eyes were the same colour—though this pair was guarded as they studied her stiff form.

He seemed to be waiting for her to do something. Make some gesture in respect of his high station maybe. But for the life of her—call it pride if you will—Evie could not offer this man any kind of gesture of respect.

Instead her chin came up, her eyes glassing over in a way Raschid would have instantly recognised if he had been here to see it happen.

His ice-princess was still alive and flourishing.

But Raschid wasn't here, and the slick way she had been separated from him had her turning those cold eyes on Ranya in accusation. The other girl's lovely cheeks flushed slightly in response, her soft lips mouthing a silent sound of apology.

'Thank you, Ranya,' Crown Prince Hashim murmured coolly. 'You may leave us.'

'No!' It was sheer self-preservation that forced the protest from Evie's throat. 'Don't leave me alone with him,' she pleaded with Ranya.

Ranya looked uncertain suddenly. 'Papa...' She turned anxious eyes on him.

'Go!' he commanded. The voice was strong, dictatorial—yet right on the back of that harsh command came a sudden weariness. 'Please, child,' he added heavily. 'Trust me. Give me some privacy to do what I have to do.'

With a rustle of silk and a touch of her hand to Evie's arm in mute apology, Ranya obeyed without further hesitation. The door closed softly behind her, leaving a stifling silence behind.

Neither moved. Neither spoke. Evie felt that tension in her back increase to tingling proportions. Once again, the Crown Prince seemed to be waiting for her to say something, but once again Evie refused to utter a word until she knew exactly what it was she was dealing with here.

'So,' he said at last. 'You are the golden icon my son was willing to forfeit his illustrious heritage for.'

'I love your son,' Evie threw back coolly. 'Too much to expect him to do anything so drastic for me.'

'A moot point,' the old man said. 'For he was prepared to do it with or without your blessing.'

'I'm—sorry if that hurt you,' Evie murmured stiffly. 'But, as you and I both know, Raschid has a mind and a will of his own.'

'Too true—too true,' he ruefully acknowledged. 'A fact that was brought home to me in the severest way possible. Call me arrogant if you wish, but I did not expect my son to defy me as he did,' he confessed. 'It came as a—shock to discover he had grown a strength of will that by far outstretched my own...'

He paused then to study her curiously, as if he was trying to discover what it was about her that had given his son such strength of will. Evie could have told him, but she was refusing to give this man anything.

Maybe he understood that. 'Still,' he shrugged. 'Who am I to complain when Raschid is proving to be the kind of man I always prayed he would become? And I am sorry for frightening you with my unfair tactics while my son taught me this salutary lesson. There,' he concluded. 'Does that clear the air between us a little?'

'Not if you've brought me here to repeat the offer,' she said.

To her surprise he smiled. And it was like watching Raschid come to life in this older version. That smile flipped her heart over. 'No.' Ruefully he shook his covered head. 'A lesson learned so painfully is usually an unforgettable one.'

He went quiet for a moment, his eyes clouding over with what Evie could only interpret as remorse. 'The child is safe?' he asked suddenly. 'Your health is quite recovered?'

Evie gave a stiff nod in reply to both questions. But

mistrust in his sincerity kept her lips tightly shut on the return query as to his own health.

His half smile told her he knew exactly why she was refusing to ask that question. 'If you give my son this much trouble when he does something you do not like, then I pity him,' he drawled. 'Please...' he then said suddenly. 'Will you come and sit?'

Evie's instinct was to refuse. She had no wish to move one inch away from this door behind which lay relative safety. But it suddenly struck her that he wasn't standing so tall as he had been—as if the strength was slowly seeping out of him.

Like his son, she realised, good manners were bred into him. Love her or hate her, he could not bring himself to sit while a lady remained standing.

And, determined though she was not to soften her feelings towards him, neither could she keep a sick man standing when it wasn't necessary. So she moved warily across the cluttered room to the other wing-backed chair set across the fireplace from the one the Prince had been sitting in when she arrived.

He waited until she sat down on the edge of it before he lowered himself carefully into the other one.

'Thank you,' he sighed, easing himself back into the chair then wearily closing his eyes.

An uncomfortable feeling of concern began to gnaw at her. 'Are you all right?' she felt constrained to ask. 'Would you like me to get someone?'

'No, no.' He refused the offer. 'I can sit, I can lie, but I must not stand for long periods,' he explained. Then his eyes suddenly flicked open, homing in like two sharp golden lances on her face. 'I offer you this information because I understand that you are loath to request it,' he said with a small wry smile that made her rather disturbingly aware of just how easily he was seeing through her.

Just like his son.

Then his eyes were suddenly darkening into true gravity. 'Despite your opinion of me, I am not a barbarian,' he grimly announced. 'I do not kill babies.'

Instantly Evie's chin came up, her lavender-blue eyes filled with damning scepticism.

'You may believe that or not.' He coolly dismissed her expression. 'For as it stands I am guilty as charged of attempting the subtle bribe to get you out of my son's life,' he admitted. 'But the other suggestion presented to you was most definitely *not* sanctioned by me.'

'Are you saying that the bed reserved in the private clinic was not your doing?' Evie questioned.

The nod of his covered head confirmed the point. 'Though I can accept,' he added, 'that I must have given the impression that it would have been better if the coming child had not been conceived or my ill-chosen messenger would not have taken the initiative upon himself to add such a grave suggestion in my name. Needless to say—' he shrugged '—Jamal Al Kareem no longer holds such a trusted position in my employ—or any other position, come to that.'

'If this is the truth, why hasn't Raschid told me all of this?' Evie was already questioning the truth in what he was saying here, for there was no doubt in her mind that Raschid would have rushed to tell her—if only to help clear his father's name.

But the Crown Prince was shaking his head. 'Raschid cannot tell you what he does not know,' he said, then added with a shrug and a grim smile, 'He would kill the man if he discovered this. Better I continue to shoulder the blame than have my son imprisoned for murder in one of our own jails. He will learn to forgive me in time, you see. Whereas you,' he added shrewdly, 'I suspect will never forgive—or even let me get close to my grandchild if you continue to believe me capable of such a dastardly crime.

Which is why, of course, I am making this confession to you.'

He was right, and Evie didn't even bother to pretend otherwise. Now all she had to do was decide whether she could risk believing him or not.

Then she looked into that face that was so like Raschid's face. Saw the pride there, saw what it was costing that pride for this man to make this confession to her, and at last felt the tension begin to ease out of her backbone.

'Your people lined our route here,' she remarked, quite out of context. 'Raschid insists they were welcoming us. Were they?'

'Yes,' he confirmed.

'And was that your doing?'

'Ah,' he said, and his smile was wry to say the least. 'I understand what you are attempting to do here. You are attempting to bestow upon me qualities I do not possess,' he perceived. 'But—I will reluctantly decline the redeeming offer. So—no.' He replied to the question. 'I did not command my people to welcome you both here tonight. In fact, I confess that their response came as big a shock to me as it did to Raschid. You see...' he added softly, 'I saw my son's marriage to you as a sign of weakness in him—whereas my people surprised me with their perception in seeing only strength in a man who stands by his principles, no matter what those principles are going to cost him.'

'Kismet,' Evie murmured softly.

'My son's definition?' he asked, then smiled. 'He could be right,' he quietly conceded. 'And who am I to be so conceited as to pull against the will of Allah?'

You are a man who is seeing your own power diminish as your son's grows stronger, Evie realised on a sharp pang of understanding as she watched those eyes so like Raschid's eyes cloud with a sadness at his own dulling senses.

And without letting herself think about it she got up and walked over to squat down beside him. 'If I promise to be as good a wife as any woman could be for your son,' she offered, 'do you think you and I could call a truce?'

'And what would you require from me in return?'

'Acceptance,' Evie answered instantly. 'That I am what Raschid wants—even though I absolutely refuse to walk two paces behind him, no matter how exalted he is,' she added with a teasing smile that at last melted the ice from her eyes.

The Crown Prince burst out laughing.

And that was how Raschid caught them when he strode into the room a moment later. His face was hard, his eyes angry, his body taut with a desire to taste someone's blood.

'Ah,' his father murmured in greeting. 'My prodigal son at last. You have married well, Raschid.' He dryly announced his approval. 'She is beautiful. She is tough, and she is blessed with compassion. I commend your good taste and your good fortune.'

'I wish you would tell me what he said to you,' Raschid sighed out in heavy frustration.

'I told you,' Evie replied, leaning contentedly against him. They were standing on the balcony of Raschid's private apartment in his father's palace. The stars were still out, though not for much longer. Dawn was on its way. 'He apologised. I accepted his apology. Then we called a truce.'

'Just like that?' He didn't believe her.

'Well, not—just like that,' she allowed, but still had no intention of breaking his father's confidence. 'I liked him,' she confessed. 'He showed dignity in defeat and apologised with grace. And I felt sorry for him,' she added with a small sigh. 'He sees his own strength fading as yours grows stronger. It hurts him.'

'And because of that you decided to forgive him?'

'Well, no. But...' Twisting around in his arms, Evie gazed up at him solemnly. 'He *is* your father,' she explained. 'Which means that without him *you* would not have been born. Now...' she continued, moving closer to the lean, hard length of his body. 'Just think for a moment what that would mean to me. No you and me coming together like this,' she said as her fingers began trailing across his silk-covered shoulders. 'No one for me to love and be loved by. No fantastic sex on a starlit balcony...'

'No, Evie,' he groaned, catching hold of her fingers. 'I—'

'I know,' she cut in. 'You made this vow. But—tell me, Raschid, how much more proof does Allah need that you must truly love me, having just watched you marry me not once, but three times? And anyway,' she went on before he could answer, 'I have come up with a really ingenious strategy to get around your silly vow,' she confided, reaching up to run the tip of her tongue along the rigid line of his jaw.

'I seduce you...' she whispered, freeing her captured fingers so she could slip the bootlace straps that were holding up her nightdress down her arms. 'You don't have to do a single thing, I promise you...' Fine silk whispered to the ground around her bare feet.

'This way, your honour remains firmly intact and I get what I want...' she explained as her hands then became busy with the belt on his blue silk robe.

She found warm, tight male flesh and pounced hungrily on it. Her body arched, stretched sensually then moved even closer until she was pressing herself to the full length of him.

'You see,' she breathed against his mouth, 'you taught me well. I know all the right moves to make this work for us...'

As she spoke one of her legs hooked itself around his leg, the pad of her bare foot stroking caressingly along a rock-solid calf muscle. The action brought her hips into more intimate contact with what was cradled between his hips.

If he was fighting to withhold his response to this blatant bit of female provocation, he wasn't being very successful, and Evie sighed with pleasure against his mouth as she moved softly against him.

It took just two minutes to make him weaken, and another two to have him scoop her up in his arms and carry her inside. The bed waited—a wickedly decadent affair with silk sheets strewn with jewel-coloured cushions, which he settled them both down amongst.

Then there were too many long, delicious minutes to count when he took over the seduction, drawing her down through layer after layer of pleasure until she lay, boneless, beneath him.

'A thousand years from now,' he murmured as he paused above her, his face a dark gold map of intense desire, 'I will still remember this night.'

'Why this night, in particular?' Evie questioned curiously. They had done this many times before after all.

'Because of—this,' he muttered, reaching out to take hold of her hand and bringing it to his mouth. 'Mine,' he breathed, taking a biting grip on her wedding ring at the same moment that he entered her.

It was such a possessive, pagan, passionate thing to do that Evie laughed as her long legs wrapped themselves around him so she could draw him in deeper.

'Barbarian,' she accused him.

It never occurred to her to question the thousand-year memory he had just laid claim to. But that was because she didn't need to. Kismet was like that—answered questions that most people would find absurd.

 **HARLEQUIN®**
*Makes any time special™*

# In celebration of Harlequin®'s golden anniversary

Enter to win a *dream!* You could win:

- A luxurious trip for two to
  *The Renaissance Cottonwoods Resort*
  in Scottsdale, Arizona, or
- A bouquet of flowers once a week for a year
  from **FTD**, or
- A $500 shopping spree, or
- A fabulous bath & body gift basket, including
  **K-tel's** *Candlelight and Romance* 5-CD set.

Look for **WIN A DREAM** flash on
specially marked Harlequin® titles by
Penny Jordan, Dallas Schulze,
Anne Stuart and Kristine Rolofson
in October 1999*.

**FTD**

**RENAISSANCE.
COTTONWOODS RESORT**
SCOTTSDALE, ARIZONA

**K·TEL**

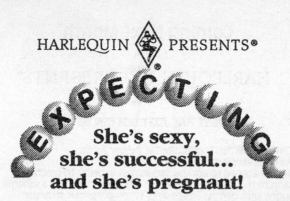

# Coming Next Month

## HARLEQUIN PRESENTS®

### THE BEST HAS JUST GOTTEN BETTER!

**#2061 THE MISTRESS ASSIGNMENT Penny Jordan**
**(Sweet Revenge/Seduction)**
Kelly has agreed to act the seductress in order to teach a lesson to the man who betrayed her best friend. It's a scheme fraught with danger—especially when gorgeous stranger Brough Frobisher gets caught in the cross fire....

**#2062 THE REVENGE AFFAIR Susan Napier**
**(Presents Passion)**
Joshua Wade was convinced that Regan was plotting to disrupt their wedding. Regan had to admit there was unfinished business between them—a reckless one-night stand.... She had good reason for getting close to Joshua, though, but she could never reveal her secret plans....

**#2063 SLADE BARON'S BRIDE Sandra Marton**
**(The Barons)**
When Lara Stevens and Slade Baron were both facing an overnight delay in an airport, Slade suggested they spend the time together. Who would she hurt if Lara accepted his invitation? He wanted her, and she wanted . . . his child!

**#2064 THE BOSS'S BABY Miranda Lee**
**(Expecting!)**
When Olivia's fiancé ditched her, her world had been blown apart and with it, her natural caution. She'd gone to the office party and seduced her handsome boss! But now Olivia has a secret she dare not tell him!

**#2065 THE SECRET DAUGHTER Catherine Spencer**
Soon after Joe Donnelly's sizzling night with Imogen Palmer, she'd fled. Now ten years on, Joe was about to uncover an astonishing story—one that would culminate in a heartrending reunion with the daughter he never knew he had.

**#2066 THE SOCIETY GROOM Mary Lyons**
**(Society Weddings)**
When Olivia meets her former lover, rich socialite Dominic FitzCharles, at a society wedding, he has a surprise for her: he announces their betrothal to the press, in front of London's elite. Just how is Olivia supposed to say no?